The Angelic Intent
Book Three in the Anarchy of Angels Trilogy

Eddie Georgonicas

Published by Rogue Phoenix Press
Copyright © 2016

978-1-62420-271-1

Credits
Cover Artist: Designs by Ms G
Editor: Kitty Carlisle

Dedication

As always, a big thank you to Carla Beer who has taken her time to offer critique and commentary. She has done so with all 3 books.

My writing of this trilogy was inspired by a childhood friendship and a loving grandmother. (Whom I dearly miss.)

Prologue

The angels had set out to collect their souls. They knew what they were doing.

Strategically and planned, it began with Mary and her husband Charlie. And then Mary's mother Pam and then her son Tony.

Tony was not alone. His best friend Johnny would be by his side.

They each had their part to play in the grander angelic plan. Each to his or her own, carrying out their heavenly duty diligently and without question.

All but the two best friends remembered.

The boys had undertaken a mission of angelic proportions. They had ventured into hell and taken on the place of fire and brimstone.

They were lucky to escape with their lives, but return to God's sacred place they did.

Heaven, in all of its power and glory, then returned the two young friends to live out their lives on Earth as it was originally intended to be. Tony and Johnny held no memory of ever having completed their angelic mission.

The heavens were proud of what the boys had accomplished, but the devil was rampant with rage. Furious he had been fooled by two mere mortals.

He sought revenge, for these two young souls had scarred the place of fire and brimstone. The boys did as the angels requested and placed the heavenly light source on the rim of Hell Central.

A heavenly light shone like emergency search beams, fanning out wide and far. It lit up the skies for all to see, forever intruding on what was once the darkness and evil of hell.

Now God's light shone well within the depths of Hades. A small and permanent reminder that heaven would always be near.

The devil would have his day.

There were evil plans in the making and so Lucifer sent one of his finest, a warrior demon called Sebastian.

The dark angel stalked the boys across the streets of Germany. No person could ever know that this warrior demon had escaped heaven to walk amongst the communities of Earth. Anything Sebastian undertook could only be done outside of prying human eyes. He had to find a way to move around incognito.

And so by ridding innocent victims of their souls and stepping in, Sebastian could take over their bodies and hide. The outer form would be human, but within lay the soul of a demon who controlled his human shell like a puppet master.

However, the human body cannot sustain its life without its soul and Sebastian quickly discovered he could only use his human host transport for a short time. The flesh of the body would begin the process of necrosis. After a little while Sebastian was left with little choice but to leave the shell of a human he possessed to then search out his next unsuspecting victim.

All in the name of revenge, to find Johnny and Tony and make them suffer.

Sebastian would possess many a human to pursue the boys. The last innocent to have his soul vacated violently was a preacher man.

Sebastian jumped into his body as quickly as putting on a winter coat. For a short time, many would never come to know that their local priest was indeed a servant from hell. A wolf in sheep's clothing.

And ironic how one who followed the holiest of lives succumbed to what one might best describe as the most unholiest of deaths.

Sebastian was without mercy as he cast the priest's soul aside. Threw his soul out like one disposes a dirty rag. He was quick to step in and play the part of a man of the cloth.

However, the only thing Sebastian was dedicated to was his mission. An undertaking handed down to him personally by Lucifer. It was Johnny and Tony that they all wanted, and they wanted them to suffer for their partaking in their angelic given mission.

Sebastian had lured the boys to within the confines of the famous gothic church in Cologne, Germany. They were not alone. Joining the boys was Liz, a talented psychic medium and two young children, Anita and Gunther.

Liz was on the ground floor behind a row of pews midway back. She was contemplating what to do next. She quickly got up and made her way to a section of the church which contained a selection of religious artefacts.

As she ran, the children were in her thoughts. They had done what was asked of them and were in hiding. The last she saw of them, they had run toward the right corner of the church, past one of the confessionals and past the stairs. Liz was comfortable and she was certain they were safe for now, well hid from demonic eyes.

She stopped to gather her breath. This part of the church had all sorts of religious artefacts, pictures and statues. Amongst all the Christian memorabilia, an ancient piece shaped like a crucifix and called the "Four Children of Christ" caught the psychic medium's immediate attention.

Meanwhile up above in one of the massive church steeples, Johnny and Tony battled with Sebastian.

Sebastian would have it no other way, for his primary mission was to ensure the boys had a first class ticket to hell…

Chapter One
The Battle in a Gothic Church
(From Book Two—*A Heavenly Interception*)

The demonic beast tried his luck with a spiritual attack and grown impatient. He gave up on the idea of destroying their souls and was now intent on doing only physical damage.

"I'm hurting," said Johnny as he tried to stand true and proud.

Tony watched as his friend struggled to maintain an upright posture. He had taken a fair beating.

Johnny looked the part of frail and weak, but that was okay because Tony would be strong for both of them.

Tony switched his attention to Sebastian and as he did, he took a step in front of his friend. Johnny kept his position to the rear, protecting his damaged limb. It was an effort to keep his boxing guard up, but that he did: left arm up and at the ready, right arm down, bloodied and bruised.

Tony put his guard up, too. He shared Johnny's attitude: if he was to be defeated he would go down with a fight.

"I'll take him. You go," said Tony.

"What? And miss all the fun! Never!" retorted Johnny. A quirky smile quickly followed.

There was nothing more to be said. The boys stood at the ready. Sebastian made his way in to attack the already wounded Johnny. He needed to walk through Tony to do so.

Tony was quick to react as he jumped into action, intercepting the attack, stepping forward and kicking the beast.

Sebastian may have intended to finish off the bruised and battered

Johnny, but Tony would never allow it. Stepping forward, he delivered a crashing, front thrust kick to the beast's jaw.

Tony then threw out a flurry of kicks and punches. It was a serious counter attack.

Many of Tony's techniques were landing on their target. He barely missed.

The demonic beast was resilient.

Sebastian stumbled back only to recover quickly. Each blow Tony delivered made his evil-bound enemy stagger back a little farther — and it took that little longer to recover.

But the devilish one gave back as much as he took. Tony defended as much as he attacked. Tony's defence tactics stopped Sebastian from hitting with full force, but his opponent was strong.

Previously, Johnny had taken the full brunt of every attack. He stood alone, face to face with an evil-spirited soul whose intent was to kill. Johnny fought his fight strength against strength. A fight he could never win.

Previously, the young fighter shook with every pounding, evil blow.

Sebastian hit hard and the injuries Johnny sustained were serious and a testament to a vicious and powerful enemy.

Now it was Tony's turn and unlike his friend, he preferred a different tact. One of deflection as opposed to standing your ground.

With well-timed movements, Tony would deviate the energy behind every strike. Sebastian could have been a hundred times stronger and that wouldn't have made a difference. As long as Tony kept his blocks well timed, he would continue to shift and deflect every bit of this brutal assault.

The demon's punches continued to be swept past the left and right of Tony's head. Tony's defence tactics were sound and well developed.

But still, even the best of fighters get hit and after a little while, the demon's attacks were to get the better of this young and competent martial artist.

Tony danced around the open area. He needed the time to recover and evasive footwork was his only way of doing so. Quick on his feet, he dodged the attempt on his life.

Tony maintained his position in front of his friend, giving Johnny the time to recover his energy levels.

The beast charged, repositioned and charged again as Tony danced around like Mohammed Ali boxing at his finest.

Johnny moved along the edge of the open platform. He was trying to keep close to his friend. Despite his injuries, he was now alert and on the ready. He would jump in with every last bit of stamina if he was needed.

Tony dodged and Johnny followed to the best of his ability, staying close as always. Sebastian lunged and missed his opponents. The demonic soldier then stopped.

There was a momentary lull.

The boys were at one end of the church steeple's viewing platform and the beast at the other. The boys kept their composure, glaring angrily at their opponent.

Three chests in a church steeple tower all heaving for fresh oxygen. Three entities whose stamina's were pushed to their very limits. Three souls fighting, determined never to give in.

Sebastian snarled, allowing a misty bloom of air to hover before it disappeared completely.

Sebastian had grown weary of Tony's footwork.

Outclassed, the demonic warrior looked for another strategy. He refocussed on Johnny, knowing Johnny couldn't move as swiftly. He walked steadily toward the wounded fighter, anticipating Tony would be ready to jump in.

Instinctively, Tony and Johnny both waited and then when the distance was right, they both went on the attack. Johnny grabbed the predator in a headlock with his good arm, trying to wrestle him to the ground. Tony took on the creature at his midsection. Sebastian's great strength did not make this an easy task. Together, the boys struggled to ground the demon.

At this moment, Liz reached the top of the stairwell with the crucifix over her back and right shoulder. The artefact "Four Children of Christ" was in her possession. She hauled the church crucifix over her shoulder in the same way Christ hauled the cross up the hill to his crucifixion.

It was a Christian artefact which held its place proudly as one of the many displays for all to enjoy. It was one of the church's most controversial and most treasured.

It was built on a wooden base formed as a large cross that stood about five feet long and three feet wide with sharpened, pointed ends all bound in the middle with some heavy twine. At each corner hung a skull which had been pierced by the thick wooden stake and left to hang just below the sharp edge. Four corners of the cross, four human skulls, looking right back at you. This crucifix had come to be known as the "Four Children of Christ" and was the only artefact in the church that was accurately traced back to the inception of Christianity itself.

How it came to be in the possession of a modern day church remained a mystery, but on this occasion, it was carried by a German psychic medium.

Madame Liz was filled with rage, furious at the beast. She looked on as the boys wrestled him down with difficulty.

"Protect the innocent," she said to herself.

Very quickly she mustered up her courage and screamed as she charged at the evil one. She still carried the cross on her back with the top stake protruding from above her right shoulder.

The screaming sound grabbed the attention of the boys. They let go of the beast and gave Liz room to do what she had to do.

Sebastian turned to face the oncoming onslaught of Liz as she ran at him. Her intent was to ram or indeed, to spear the enemy.

Sebastian took the full brunt of the attack rolling back as he was pierced by the wooden stake. The sharpness of the stake and the holiness of the relic combined to inflict the damage necessary to bring this creature of darkness to his end.

As Sebastian rolled backward, Liz tumbled forward. The upper end of the cross lodged itself in the rib cage of the beast.

As he fell, the bottom of the cross rotated up like a fulcrum. And as the cross rotated, it flicked Liz up into a rolling tumble. She landed at the other end of the cross.

The beast was now impaled by the top of the cross and Liz's ribcage was pierced by its side arm. A human and a creature from the depths of hell both sharing a place on a Christian relic. Their faces only a few feet apart.

Sebastian lay motionless. He was dead and his soul had now left for the spiritual plane.

The psychic medium faced the physical form of the beast. She stared at his closed eyes and then used her psychic insight to look up and across to any spirits, ghosts, souls or angels in the room.

She saw a solitary archangel.

She stared at Michael with peaceful eyes. He was standing in the spiritual plane before her. He restrained the ghostly form of Sebastian as a police officer would a common criminal.

The demonic beast was no match for the archangel Michael. Liz smiled and the archangel smiled back. A second later he was gone— and so was the evil spirit of Sebastian.

Suddenly, two familiar ghostly faces were in view. The spirits of Tony's parents, Mary and Charlie stood together in their spiritual world. They half smiled at Liz. Their look said it all: they were waiting for her.

Tony ran over to Liz with Johnny not far behind. They didn't know what to do.

Suddenly and unexpectedly, the church doors opened below. The crowd rushed inside. Anita and Gunther saw their father, Josef, and ran to the safety of his arms.

All those downstairs were oblivious to the goings on up above.

Meanwhile up in the church steeple tower, Liz turned to Johnny and Tony. In her weakened state she spoke.

"You must swear to me. Two things I ask of you."

"Anything," said Tony. The young man conveyed his eternal gratitude with only a loving look and gentle smile.

"I do not want Anita and Gunther to see me like this."

"Of course," replied Tony.

"Secondly," Liz said as she gulped for another breath of air. She looked at Mary and Charlie, who nodded their heads in acknowledgement. She reached out for the hands of the two young men.

They were keen to offer her whatever comfort they possibly could.

"This is not to be discussed. You must never speak a word of this to anyone." Liz then paused as the pain from the stake suddenly became unbearable. After a small moment that seemed like an eternity for her, she turned back to the boys.

"Promise me!" she said with pain and discomfort in her voice.

"It will remain with us," replied Johnny. As he made this promise to Liz, the gypsy Madame shut her eyes forever.

At that moment, a misty cloud formation appeared before the boys. Tony's parents and Liz stood side by side in ghostly, but recognisable forms.

Charlie had his arm around Mary as he stood by her side. Mary delivered one final loving gesture to the boys. She clasped her hands together and placed them over her heart line, signifying the love she wished to share with Tony and his loyal friend.

Charlie stood by her side as proud as any father could be. Madame Liz looked like she was at peace with her passing, as she looked at the boys for one final time from beyond the other side. The three ghostly entities walked toward the two young men, stepping right through their physical beings.

The boys felt a sudden warmth and then simultaneously, they gasped for air, as if they had surfaced from a deep ocean dive.

The ghostly vision was gone. Mary and Charlie left the boys with one last gift: the ability to remember, but to not be mentally anguished by their experiences in the church steeple tower.

Despite their gruelling ordeal, the boys were now at inner peace.

Chapter Two
The Day of a Thousand Deaths

Archangel Michael left the church setting ages before. It was a scene that was upsetting to the archangel mainly because another innocent human soul had died for the sake of a demonic beast on the prowl.

Michael stood on the heavenly planes with Sebastian in a choke hold.

Typically, a soul that re-enters heaven would be confused, tired and in need of heaven's calmness. But not for one as sinister as Sebastian. The hatred he had for everything godly had been burnt into his soul for over an eternity.

The demon snarled and wriggled violently in an attempt to break free. Michael wasted no time in inflicting pain so severe, Sebastian would soon stop any attempt to break the stronghold of a warrior class angel.

Sebastian was no match for Michael and the archangel was is no mood for demonic antics. There was no further attempt to escape and for now, Sebastian was on his best behaviour.

The archangel's thoughts turned to Madame Liz. He left the spirits of Mary and Charlie behind and they would soon take care of a psychic medium who sacrificed herself for the greater purpose.

With the beast subdued and calm, the archangel spread his swan-like wings. As he did, he loosened his muscular grip enough to keep his stronghold on Sebastian firm, but not overly tight.

Sebastian twisted his head enough to see the massive wingspan of the archangel. They stretched out to a little over six feet. Impressively large, feathery and as white as snow.

Michael stood his ground. He reflected on a friendly soul by the name of Madame Liz. She was indeed a gifted psychic medium whose spiritual insight was unique. There was no-one in the world quite like her.

This lady was special to Michael and the angelic hierarchy, for throughout her lifetime, the Angels provided Madame Liz with the psychic wisdom to help guide people's lives.

More importantly, she carried out this task as diligently and professionally as any could expect. She went above and beyond her duty to mankind and to the heavens above.

Michael had borne witness many a time to the personal sacrifice she made in order to help others.

And now, Madame Liz, a psychic medium, lay pierced on the artefact cross. She would soon cross over to become one of heaven's valued members. That he knew for sure.

This beast had rid the Earth of a talented medium that could have helped so many more. The Earth, or at least Madame Liz's part of it, would never be the same again.

The anger built up inside the archangel. So many good souls had died with Sebastian's rampage on Earth.

Michael would have choked the spiritual life out of Sebastian, but this was not the way of a loving archangel. Michael pushed aside these feelings, for he dare not let hatred get the better part of him.

Michael stood his ground a little longer. He was angry, but in control.

Sebastian grew restless. The demonic one was no longer wriggling in an attempt to escape, but more so in an attempt to get comfortable.

Michael could wait no longer. He would have to leave Liz's entrance into heaven to the capable hands of the spirits of Charlie and Mary.

There was heavenly business to attend to. There was a hell-born beast that needed heaven's rehabilitation. The need to convert the evil spirit of Sebastian to one of a loving heavenly entity would be underway soon.

And besides, Michael did not want to spend any more moments in heaven with a beast attached to his forearm.

"Walk, you demon!" demanded Michael.

Michael walked with a crouched over demon in a headlock type grip. Sebastian did the best he could to comply and he did not resist.

Michael walked a little longer as Sebastian struggled to keep up with the pace of the great angel. This made Michael's walking look a little awkward as he dragged one of hell's finest behind him.

Michael saw his angelic friends ahead. Archangel Gabriel and angel Raphael were in the presence of the great seraphim angel, Zophiel.

Michael walked up to the group of angels, but in particular, sought the presence of Zophiel.

Zophiel stood taller than the angels around him, reaching almost nine feet in height. His main torso was serpent-like and attached to his rubbery-like, solid frame were six large, leathery, bat-like wings. A brightness shone from his face, bearable to angels, but not so to souls and spirits. One could not look upon the great angel for any length of time as his was a face that shone with God's light.

Zophiel had the legs of a muscular human and arms that were more fitting on a giant grizzly bear. He had the claws to match.

"I have the demon. How would you like for me to proceed?" asked Michael.

Gabriel and Raphael left the conversation, leaving Michael and Zophiel to sort out their future plans for Sebastian.

Zophiel gestured and Michael handed over his prisoner. Sebastian wriggled again in an attempt to escape. He screeched and screamed and suddenly became more agitated and aggressive.

Without further hesitation, Zophiel ripped the demon apart. This was not about physical death, for that part had occurred in the upper level of a church steeple tower. Back then, Sebastian had taken on physical form and had met his demise.

Now it was time to terminate his spiritual form.

And as quick as that, Sebastian had died and under the law of heaven, would return to the place of light and love to be rehabilitated.

"Fetch me Sebastian," asked the seraphim angel of his friend Michael.

Without question, Michael flew off to a corner of heaven to find the diabolical one cowered in a lonely part of a white, billowy, misty floor. He was in shock from his sudden and unexpected death. Michael grabbed the demon and was quick to return to Zophiel.

It didn't take the archangel long to return with a dazed and somewhat confused demonic soldier in his possession.

"As you requested," stated Michael.

Zophiel walked up to Sebastian and without notice, ripped him apart again. The screech was brief and eerie. The deafening crack of the evil spirit dying was sharp, succinct and typical of any spiritual death.

No matter what the spiritual entity, be it angel or demon, the dying of a spiritual soul all sounds the same.

Michael looked up at Zophiel. He was puzzled and could no longer keep his silence.

He asked his friend, speaking only a singular word, "Why?"

Zophiel was quick to reply. "The demon is as sinister as they come. To rehabilitate his soul would be wasteful of our resources. This I am certain of. Sebastian is unlikely to convert. Please fetch me his soul, I will explain when you return."

Michael trusted in the wisdom of his seraphim friend. There was no doubting his word. The archangel was off again and soon returned with a startled and shocked Sebastian in his hands.

The demonic beast was somewhat dazed, as if he had taken a strong right cross in the fifteenth round of a boxing match, but the fact of the matter was that Michael had laid no hands on Sebastian.

The shock of a sudden death is disturbing to any type of spiritual entity. The shock of two sudden and unexpected deaths within minutes could not even be comprehended.

Sebastian was lost in his own world of mental anguish. He would need the time to comprehend not one, but two unexpected deaths in the matter of a handful of minutes.

Zophiel walked up to Sebastian. As he did, Michael let go of his prisoner and let the seraphim do what he had to do. Zophiel was quick to rip the demon apart. Once again a brief and sharp shriek followed by the deafening crack of spiritual death.

"I will shock his body a thousand times over. A thousand deaths. No time to recover. I will torture his spiritual soul in a way that I have never done before. Only then will we stand a chance of rehabilitating one as evil as he in mindset. He is one of Lucifer's finest soldiers, so I will truly put his soul through hell before I even attempt to convert him into our heavenly ways." Zophiel could see no other way.

Zophiel turned to Michael.

"We are going to be here for a while, my friend. Please fetch me his soul."

Chapter Three
The Pyramid of Heaven

Zophiel was a little over half way through his task. At five hundred and fifty six deaths, he waited for Michael to return with Sebastian in his hands, once again.

Soon after, the archangel had flown in carrying a limp and, what looked like lifeless body of Sebastian.

The archangel laid his body down softly. Sebastian, worn out and incredibly lethargic, lay flat out on the misty, billowy floor. The demon lay silent and motionless.

Zophiel looked to his friend.

"What is it?" he asked compassionately.

Michael paused for a few seconds before replying.

"I believe and trust in your wisdom, Zophiel, but it troubles me to witness such cruelty. This is not our way. We are a place of peace and love. Even this demon does not deserve such torturous methods."

Zophiel empathised and nodded accordingly, but he did not reply. He remained silent as he turned to watch over his prisoner. He observed the evil soldier who had only recently mustered the energy to sit up. Sebastian looked the part of a mindless soul.

Sebastian looked to the sky of blue. Where one would instantly warm to the love and beauty of heaven's skyline, the prisoner watched on with no reaction whatsoever.

Zophiel then turned to face Michael. It was time his archangel friend understood why it was necessary to do what had to be done.

"Sebastian was not born a demonic leader, but he was groomed into one. Lucifer saw potential, dedication and loyalty in his prized General. The devil made Sebastian into his own ways. Memories, experience, personal beliefs and personal life values. What became important to Lucifer was now even more important to Sebastian. The demonic soldier follows his leader blindly and unconditionally. This is a mindset so dedicated and so evil. And so I am left with little choice. I rip it apart. Destroy it!"

At that point, Zophiel made the gesture with his hands like tearing a piece of invisible paper in two and then tossing both pieces away.

"But the challenge still remains. Sebastian is returned to me and it is only a matter of time before he recreates his former self. This I am certain of. His memories and life experiences will return to him and he will eventually become the evil soul he once was."

Zophiel continued. "And try as we will, to convert one who has spent an eternity in a place of fire and brimstone is asking the impossible, even from the most patient of angels. So I need to start again. Mix up the memories, the experiences and the beliefs and values he holds so close to his demonic heart."

The seraphim paused for a second. He then spoke his final sentence with authority and conviction. He didn't like speaking directly to his friend, but his point needed to be made.

"So I tear him apart again!"

Zophiel walked to Sebastian and thrust his muscular, human-like leg into his chest. The demon hit heaven's floor with a solid thump. The great seraphim angel kept his leg on Sebastian, who struggled for a short time and then gave into the fact he was not going to sit up until his captor moved away.

Zophiel continued as he looked straight at his helpless victim.

"His blank mind now a dry sponge ready to re-absorb every evil memory. It takes time to re-organise the experiences of an evil lifetime, but re-establish himself, he will. The mess in his demonic mind will begin to take shape. He will eventually take on his former thoughts and life events and as such will return to his former self. But after every death little bits do get lost. Left out as it were. Sebastian is not the creature now that he once was. Five hundred and fifty six times will do this to you. What starts out as an empty mind will be refilled with thoughts belonging to a lifetime of evil ways. This is the way of rehabilitation. I know you have experienced it as have I, but only once over. We had the time to recover. Sebastian never will. I'll repeat the process and terminate his life force time and time again."

Zophiel stopped and pointed at Sebastian's face. He wished nothing more than to highlight the point.

"At five hundred and fifty six deaths later and my plan has taken effect. I can see the process of reinstalling demonic memories is totally chaotic. It is taking its toll on him. The memories are re-entering the demon's mindset scrambled. Slowly but surely, Sebastian is losing bits of his identity. By the time I get him to a thousand deaths, the demonic memories are hopefully so jumbled, that we in heaven have something to work with. A naked mindset which is receptive to our ways. A mindset for which to wipe out the old and re-install with the new."

The seraphim angel carefully considered his next move.

Zophiel's strength was impressive. He could take his foot off and reach down for him at any time. Rip him apart in a split second, but instead, the great seraphim angel paused for a little longer.

He lifted his foot and allowed Sebastian to sit up. The evil one stared blankly into the sky and Zophiel held back on killing him for the five hundredth and fifty seventh time.

For a moment, Michael and Zophiel simultaneously gazed upon the demon like he was an injured animal in distress.

"I understand, but I can't help but feel pity for him," said Michael.

"Have you forgotten, my friend," replied Zophiel. "How many innocents did he sacrifice in the name of his own personal evil cause? His recent venture on Earth left a path of destruction we still have to deal with here in heaven. Have no pity on his soul, but work with me to make him a loving and giving member of heaven's community."

Zophiel could not kill until the process of memory re-installation had occurred. The signs were not there yet.

Suddenly and unexpectedly, Zophiel swung his head around. A message was being sent from a place located several stories up above. Heaven was a place of levels and hierarchy and if heaven were a pyramid, then the origins of this message were coming directly from the top.

Zophiel looked back at the demon that looked like he had only just awoken from a long and blissful sleep. Zophiel turned to his angelic friend and then paused for a moment longer as he raised his muscular human-like legs and thrust them down on Sebastian's chest once again.

Sebastian fell back onto the misty floor of heaven with an even louder thud than the time before. Zophiel had made his point clear. He did not want Sebastian going anywhere until he returned.

"I must leave, I am being summoned. I must speak with God immediately. I will be back shortly"

"What would you like me to do?" asked Michael.

"Let the demon be. Do not do anything until I return, but he is not to leave this place."

"Understood!" replied Michael.

Zophiel took off, leaving Michael to stand over Sebastian. Zophiel took to the sky and flew higher and higher into the levels of heaven.

The ground from which he had left was reserved for all souls, spirits, angels and any spiritual entity that wished to walk and mingle. As one flew up from the common grounds of heaven, then one was exposed to the levels where the higher order of angels resided.

Up in the plane above was reserved for the angels and archangels. Here was the greatest number of pure spirits by far. Protectors of heaven and mediators between man on Earth, and spirit and angel in heaven. This hierarchy of angels helped with the transition into heaven and they delivered their guidance to those on Earth.

This level was not restricted and often souls and spirits ventured between common ground to that of the higher level of angel and archangel.

Above them, on the next plane was choir, dominions, thrones, powers, cherubim, principalities. All had their place and function to God and to the angelic intent.

Higher still was a place restricted for seraphims that were considered the right hand of God. This level was way above the grounds of heaven's floor. Aside from seraphim, this was also the place for Christ and the Virgin Mother.

And then the one above was the holiest of levels with only God himself, sitting at the top.

On this occasion, Zophiel had a calling to meet with God. The throne of the creator located way up high. If heaven was like Earth, then above the clouds was where God reigned.

The seraphim thrust his powerful bat-like wings.

He went higher and higher and would soon be there.

Down below, Archangel Michael observed Sebastian. The demon sat back up and regained some awareness. The demon looked at angel and the angel looked back at the demon.

A stare of minutes. Michael's face showed the smile and love only a true angel could exhibit and for a while, Sebastian replied similarly.

But as garbled sinister thoughts re-entered the mind of the evil one. As a life of damnation began to take and reform in Sebastian's subconscious, then the smile was replaced with sinister looks. He damned the angel through the stare from his beady black eyes.

The early signs were there. Sebastian began the process of re-learning of his existence. The teachings were in their infancy, but nevertheless, the process of rehabilitation had begun.

If Zophiel were present, then at this specific point, he would rip the demon apart, but as instructed, Michael simply kept close vigil.

The archangel stood and extended his swan-like wings. The demon snarled and hissed at the archangel.

"Know thy place, demon. Silence or Be Silenced!" shouted Michael with a booming voice more deafening than a roaring jumbo jet engine.

The archangel stood tall and sounded impressively strong.

The demon quickly quivered in his own private little corner like a scared puppy. The differentiation was quickly made. And so there Michael stood until Zophiel returned soon after.

As soon as Zophiel landed, the beast snarled at the fresh face, quickly forgetting the instructions from the archangel. Zophiel wasted no time and walked up to him as he had done so may a time before. For the five hundredth and fifty seventh time he ripped the beast in half.

The shriek and cracking sound familiar.

Michael was off without instruction to fetch his prisoner.

Zophiel, now standing alone, had the time and looked up.

God's words were sitting uneasy within the great seraphim, for he had learnt Lucifer would have his day and this day was near.

19

God could foresee it and there was nothing anyone could do about it. However, the one thing asked of the great seraphim was disturbing to him even more.

Zophiel could not speak or share of his knowledge of the coming event and so he was left with little choice but to unreservedly put his faith into God's instructions.

Chapter Four
Lucifer's Army

The devil had his spy. Word had got back to him long ago.

Sebastian was captive in a heaven that would not stop. One way or another, God's kingdom would find a way to convert one of Lucifer's finest and dedicated warriors.

The devil sat on his rock of solitude, the throne to the kingdom of evil.

Lucifer was grand in presence and his rocky throne was fitting to this grandeur.

The seat stood high and tall. It was carved with engravings and scriptures of evil. Over the millennia, this was the place where the devil pondered, plotted or devised his cunning plans. Plans to steal a soul, a plan to convert an angel, attack heaven or wage wrongfulness on mankind.

But today, his thoughts were on one. The plan had been executed and was in the making. Its beginnings were about to take shape. This was a mission of rescue.

The round the clock torture of his prized General Sebastian was unacceptable. Heaven had had their way for far too long.

Lucifer was determined. Sebastian would be returned to his rightful home to take his place in the demonic ranks.

Lucifer sat on his throne as he watched on, all around and surrounding the evil emperor, foot soldiers snarled and snickered on the open and dark fields of Hades while dark angels flew above. They flapped hard and flew in a diabolical fashion.

The darkest of demons, the snarls and screeches was their language, understood only by those who served the devil.

Every foot soldier, every demon, every dark angel was mustered. The skies and grounds of Hell Central were now a giant blanket of grey and black. For as far as the eye could see, it was one able bodied warrior after another.

There was no formation, only packed together as comfortably tight as possible. Hundreds of thousands upon hundreds of thousands, on the ground and in the skies above.

Lucifer's thoughts were on the battle ahead. He had never attacked heaven with such great numbers. His aerial and foot army was impressively gigantic.

He stood from his throne making his way through the masses before him.

The march toward the Transitional Border and then onto Heaven Central was about to begin and Lucifer would lead the way.

The crowds below were snickering and snarling. The flying demons stopped their acrobatics only to hover up above. They flapped their wings hard. They bounced and jockeyed in the air above whilst they maintained an almost stationary position, waiting for the order to proceed.

The devil cut through his crowd. He glanced back at his troops one last time. The sea of abled warriors and flying dark angels went for as far as the eye could see. He could not be certain of the outcome, but what he could depend on was a determination to win.

Lucifer turned and took his first step and then walked onward. They collectively moved with him toward their unsuspecting target. Lucifer at the lead with his entire population behind him.

Heaven would hopefully be caught off guard.

And as sure as there was fire and brimstone in hell, the following was a certainty. For in years to come, this great battle would go down in the history books of both heaven and hell. In a distant future, demon and angel alike would look back and refer to the war ahead in much the same way.

It's opening day, to be famously remembered as a time that made God weep.

Chapter Five
At War

Close to five Earth years passed and all the time, the battle raged within heaven. God's light was not comforting to the devil and his gang, but they had fought hard and come too far to give up now.

Archangel Michael led the defensive. His angels and spiritual friends fought against the dragon and the dragon and his dark army fought back.

In recent times, the fighting had come to a standoff. Heaven's occupants retreated to the first level above. There they all held their land and stood strong, gazing down like workers at their upper storey office window onto the street below.

The dark one now controlled heaven's ground floor and had freed his trusted Sebastian from those who lived in God's care.

Off to the distant horizon, a few demons strayed away from the sight of many. They were sharing their sinister laughs and snickering in their clicks and squawks. The four evil ones had been friends for a lifetime and had taken some time out to enjoy one another's company. This was their mistake; the angels would not miss the opportunity.

Ten angels swarmed down like hailing rain. In their numbers, the kill was swift. They retreated back to higher and safer grounds. This was a small but strategic victory. Heaven would be taken back, bit by little bit if necessary.

But for the most part, Lucifer had his eyes in the skies and his feet planted firmly on God's land. With that, the devil also had the privilege to greet all newly deceased and to affect the character of the living.

Now that heaven had a different type of leader, how would a ruler filled with such nastiness affect Earth's humanity and culture?

Only time would tell, but for now, Lucifer was determined to not miss any opportunity to recruit as many souls as possible. Both the living below and newly deceased were prime targets and the devil tried to convert them into his own sadistic ways whenever the occasion called for it.

With the freshly deceased, it was a race. Where would the soul appear and who would get to it first? And the advantage here remained with the heavens as, for the most part, they knew where to look.

As was the case, a newly arrived soul appeared in a lonely part of heaven. He was a middle aged American who had lived a good life, but had not looked after his health. His heart gave up on him at the tender age of forty nine.

It was about to begin. This was the process of re-living one's memories. The man looked to the skies above in preparation of watching a lifetime of wonderful and life changing moments. Here was a good soul, a giving man.

As it had always been with the recently departed, the blue sky became the man's personal panoramic theatre. A backdrop from which to gaze upon and relive critical points in his life. Reflect on all that was.

As the blue sky began to play for the former U.S. citizen, Archangel Gabriel swooped the gentleman off his feet and airlifted him to the safety of the level above.

The procedures and practices which once existed for the newly deceased had all changed. Reflecting on one's life was no longer of primary importance; however, salvaging his soul for an eternal place in God's loving family was.

The angels wished it could be said that they always succeeded. That all souls were saved from an afterlife of fire and brimstone, but unfortunately, they retrieved as many as they lost.

However, this was the unwritten law. The angels never gave in and they certainly never, ever stopped trying.

Who controlled the grounds of heaven was in charge of incoming fresh souls and had the greater capacity to influence those who walked the earth and could, in small and sometimes big ways, change earthbound communities for better or for worse.

In summation, thy will as it were in heaven will eventually flow onto Earth, regardless of whether its primary source is good or evil.

While the higher order of angels worked from high above in their pyramid-like structure, they did their best to neutralise wavelengths of sinister origins and replace them with frequencies of love and nurture. They did all they could to make sure mankind was not swayed by subliminal messages, laced with evildoings.

Equally, on the level where angels and archangels roamed, they did their part to retrieve the freshly deceased or wage battle on Lucifer's army whenever some strayed from the main group.

War was over and now it was a time for countermeasures. A game of spiritual chess currently at a stalemate.

Which side would make their next dramatic move?

Chapter Six
A Famous Television Show

The devil was pleased with Sebastian's progress. It had taken a long time, but the General had healed and recovered to his former self. The prized demonic warrior now stood by Lucifer in order to continually defend against God's land from being retaken.

~ * ~

A news and current affairs television show called "Today, Tomorrow and Yesterday" had first introduced itself in the early nineteen seventies. Its origin began in the U.S. and by year nineteen ninety, it had grown in popularity, with many countries adapting their own version of the current news affair show.

Sometimes their stories were shared globally, played on air, for all of Today, Tomorrow and Yesterday's audience could catch up on stories of worldly interest. Other times it was one of reporting on topics of local importance only to be played on air in no other country other than the host nation of the journalistic piece.

Either way, whether the story was of a local telecast only or beamed across the world for everyone to know, their episodes were widely enjoyed by all walks of life.

Tonight was one of those local stories. It was only broadcast on the televisions of Australia.

This segment had been put together and was told by a veteran female journalist. She joined the Australian version of the show two years prior and to her credibility, had been in her chosen field of journalism for close to eighteen years.

Her face was a familiar one amongst the viewers of her native country.

Tonight, for a Sunday evening viewing, was a fifteen minute entertaining article titled "The Faith Debate—Can science and religion happily co-exist?"

It was unknown to the journalist at the time, but the trends and patterns she was reporting on could be seen across the globe, particularly in those countries that had strong and well developed Christian communities. However, the reporter was oblivious to worldly trends and tonight's show simply focussed on her research in her own country of Australia.

Henry and Tess appeared on the screens. Both were aged in their mid-forties and were talking about their history with their church.

In their early thirties they were born again Christians. They were married in a Pentecostal church in the suburbs of Adelaide and belief became the cornerstone of their lives.

The camera focussed in on Tess, her head occupying much of the television screen. She had short blonde hair that hung straight and flat, stopping a fraction below her chin line.

"I prayed a lot. It was like twenty four / seven around the clock," said Tess. "I was always talking to God and I would believe that God was talking back to me," she confessed.

The Pentecostal church was distinguished by the belief that those who served in her were baptised with the Holy Spirit. This enabled a Pentecostal Christian to live a Holy Spirit-filled and sanctioned life. This empowered life allowed followers of the faith to perform divine healings and speak in a strange dialect, commonly referred to as tongues.

Henry and Tess and their three children were baptised, and like other worshippers, they began to speak in tongues.

"When you initially do it, it's very powerful," said Henry. "You might have five or six people around you going: 'SPEAK, SPEAK, SPEAK!' Eventually you just try it. And just do it."

The camera took a close up shot of Henry's face as he proceeded to demonstrate 'tongues' by speaking a bit of gibberish. He carried on for ten or so seconds to make his point.

Henry then spoke about his family's association with the church when they were in their late thirties and early forties, by which time they had become church leaders. Tess in particular had something akin to a revelation.

The camera pulled up on Tess again.

"The first moment that really shook my world, my faith, was when I asked the question," Tess paused for a moment as she glanced at her husband who was sitting at the interview right beside her. The camera panned back to capture both husband and wife, seated side by side.

Tess then looked back at the camera whilst Henry kept his eyes fixed on his talking wife.

"What is changing through my prayer?" she asked of herself out aloud for the Australian audience to hear.

And then she proceeded to answer her own question.

"I really had to look and be honest with myself and say, 'Not a lot.'"

Henry sat next to his wife, nodding his head up and down. The movement was subtle, but noticeable none-the-less.

Tess continued saying, a nervousness evident within her gentle voice, "And that day, I just looked at Henry and I said, 'You know what? I don't believe this anymore.'"

The following words were spoken directly to her husband. At that moment in time, Tess turned her head to face him.

"I felt like someone had died. It was a real grief."

Henry nodded his head in agreement much the same way as he had done before, subtly yet noticeable.

The camera then shot to another scene. The female Australian reporter was walking in a green and well-manicured parkland.

She spoke whilst in the backdrop, the parks greenery was broken up by a young child, running to its mothers waiting arms.

The popular journalist stood in full shot talking into her microphone.

"The family decided they no longer believed in God, and they took the difficult step of leaving the church."

The scene was now back to the husband and wife, side by side as it had originally been set. Henry was speaking this time.

"People we had known, loved, had relationships with for many years, overnight, cut us off. The people we thought were our friends could no longer accept that for us, everything in science and in nature now leads me and my family not to believe anymore. But our friends can't accept us for who we are; however, we have never ever tried to persuade them out of their beliefs. We have always taken them for who they are." The hurt and sadness came through in his voice. It was evident Henry missed the people who once were an important part of his life.

"Unfortunately, we had to move on without them." This was the last thing Henry spoke before the television screen went to a giant graph.

The axis on the graph was displaying some statistics that stemmed the course of the last ten years. Starting at nineteen eighty and finishing with nineteen ninety.

The female reporter's voice came over the speakers, the chart still flickering in front of the many viewers of tonight's broadcast.

"Over the last ten years, atheism has been flourishing, with a little over a third of Australians now claiming no religion on the annual government census. Additionally, the proportion of Christians has fallen from almost ninety percent to around sixty percent."

As these words were spoken, the graphical representation on everyone's screen was drawn out and plotted. The chart had at one end the year, nineteen eighty and ran across to the far right spanning a length of the period in question. The horizontal axis highlighted the percentage of Australians who held any sort of Christian belief. The line sloped downwardly to an end point, stopping a little above the sixty percentile mark.

The interview then turned to the former chief scientist of Australia, Professor Eddie Perkins who opened his appearance with the statement, "All the major unknowns of existence are all scientific questions. I believe science and religion are not incompatible. We'll never be able to explain everything. There's a principle that says as soon as you observe something, you change it."

The scene then switched to make the ironic point. Professor Eddie was filmed playing the church organ for the Sunday congregation of his church. The camera stayed on this setting for a little while, hearing the organ play and the preacher preach, all along with Eddie Perkins concentrating on his music and then on the words of his pastor. Eddie was not fanatical, but he enjoyed his regular Sunday church gathering.

The camera scene switched again, back to the original interview with the professor. This story was concluded with Eddie's final statement.

"And besides," he said, "science will never know and never be able to answer the question of, 'Is there something more?'"

~ * ~

The devil had his spies on Earth and Australia was not immune to them. One in particular watched this interview with keen interest, well aware of the situation in heaven above.

His thoughts were on Lucifer and the news he must get to him. For the devil's efforts were not in vain. Lucifer and his demonic followers were making their impact on the Earth below.

This popular news television show was a testament to the fact.

For fewer and fewer people were becoming interested in leading a life which had faith in a holy God and a belief in a heavenly afterlife.

The devil would be pleased.

Chapter Seven
Johnny's Priesthood

Johnny and Tony witnessed things not of this world. They had fought with a beast from hell in a Cologne church steeple. That was close to seven years ago.

Back then, the encounter ended with a ghostly appearance of Tony's dead parents standing next to Liz, a recently deceased spiritual medium.

Madame Liz, a gifted psychic, had been killed by the demonic warrior, Sebastian. Tony and Johnny had only met her an hour or so before her death and yet, she sacrificed her life in order to save theirs.

Tony and Johnny kept their promise to Liz and never spoke a word about their experience with the demon or of the events that followed after the battle in the church steeple tower.

Since that day, the impressions left with Johnny had him seek a life within the church.

Since returning from Germany, Johnny could speak of nothing else, for he was consumed with a passion for dedicating himself to becoming a man of the cloth. He felt with absolutely no reservation, this had become his life's calling.

It came as a surprise to Johnny's family, but not to Tony. If only Johnny's parents knew what the boys had been through. Either way, Johnny had the unconditional support of his entire family and close friends.

Upon his return from overseas, Johnny spent the next twelve months actively attending and participating in his local church.

This was his first test. And at the end of it, he hadn't changed his mind.

Immediately after in the next five to six years, Johnny lived amongst the poor and homeless, studied philosophy and theology, got involved in the university campus ministry as well as his local church and did further studies to complete his Masters of Divinity.

All along, Tony kept up his studies as well. His field of interest was in the physical and mechanical sciences. Whilst their respective degrees may have been worlds apart, the two friends supported each other through the hectic times and pressures. It was all a part of dedicating oneself to further tertiary studies, learnings and examinations.

Many years on and Johnny was seeking approval to be ordained, the final 'test' of whether or not he had a vocation to the priesthood. It had been a long journey of several years and countless hours. Charity work, studies and selfless acts of helping and counselling the needy and the poor.

Regardless of Johnny's commitment, being ordained was something the church bishop would decide.

Johnny demonstrated his dedication to helping and to his faith, he hungered for his profession in the priesthood and the bishop had no reason to doubt him.

Johnny took his vows and graduated with honours. Tony did as well, graduating as a mechanical engineer. His paper was graded with top marks.

Located nearby was a simple looking church. Red bricked with one white cross on a single steeple that wasn't much higher than the building's roofline. The cathedral was large enough to seat a hundred or so comfortably. A relatively small place of worship, but it held a strong local following.

Its denomination was Catholic and its priest of many years announced his pending retirement. Johnny had become a part of its congregation during his university years. The current pastor and Johnny were friends. The father would hand over his position without reservation.

The building, the people, their faith, the preaching; this would soon be Johnny's to look after.

Chapter Eight
Another Side of War

God exists as does the devil.

And for us people living in the human form of existence - no matter how long we are given to walk the Earth, our very destiny, our life purpose and the footprint we leave behind, will largely depend on which we elect to follow.

~ * ~

The white billows of clouds continued to roll around heaven's floor. At ankle height, this inert entity provided a warmth and comfort to those who followed in God's light.

But now, even the misty floor was in a somewhat agitated state. Its usual smoothly rolling and embracing actions were now replaced with small, fast, agitated movements as if it was being violently pulled in one direction and then jerked in another.

The billowy mist was not a living entity, but it had been given a duty of care. In its own peculiar way, it anxiously looked for something or somebody so that it might do its eternally given job of providing healing and God-given love.

Alas, these properties were simply wasted on demon and devil. These creatures were not of this world and yet here they were, in their massive numbers, teasing and upsetting the natural balance that once existed in heaven.

Sebastian walked, cutting through the puffs of white cloud below. He was organising something he had done only twice before. It took a bit of time to get everyone behind it, but in his opinion, it was worth every bit of effort.

His task was nearly complete and for it to start, he would have to take up centre position.

All demonic troops and dark angels were standing on heaven's floor, gathered in one enormous circle. They were packed and in a comfortably tight formation.

Sebastian walked and walked, approaching his position near enough to middle. Swarming all around him were his demonic troops, too massive in number to count.

He looked up to the higher platforms of heaven. Glimpses of angels and souls could be seen at a mid-distance.

Sebastian led the way. He snarled and snickered and cursed all that was above him. He looked up and he let the upper layers of heaven have it.

Seconds later, he was joined by the full scale of all of the devil's soldiers. All around him, they began.

The sounds were booming and deafening. They taunted their heavenly counterparts. Screamed at them; sinful chants in their evil language of clicks, screams and snarly growls.

This went on for some time, until heaven gave back. The angelic screams came from above, directed to the enemy below.

Their angry angelic voices boomed. If the enemy were human, the sound waves would have shattered the skull into hundreds of fragments. This was louder than anything any human could imagine.

The demonic sound waves pulsated upwardly. The angelic screams rained downwardly and this continued for some time. A screaming argument of sorts done on the most massive of scales.

As the snarls and snickers continued, Sebastian stopped and began his walk toward the outer rim of the circle, dodging and squeezing through demonic soldier after demonic soldier.

He weaved in and out as he listened to them all scream out aloud.

His job was done and he now wished to escape the gathered troops.

With a sinister smirk on his demonic face, Sebastian let out with a brief snicker to himself.

There was always time for psychological warfare.

Chapter Nine
The Helping Spirits of Charlie and Mary Papageorgiou

Mary, in her living years, put her mother through hell. She wasn't a bad daughter. In fact, quite the opposite. She was as loving, supportive and as close to her mother as any could be.

The hell referred to was not of Mary's doing, nor of her choice, but rather, one of the circumstances at hand. And at every point, whether Mary could see it at the time or not, her mother Pam was there to pick up the pieces and hold the family unit together.

Later on, it came as no surprise to Mary that in the afterlife, the angels would choose Pam as a healer and heavenly counsellor of sorts. It came more naturally to Pam than any medico or counsellor Mary had come across on all of her Earthly existence.

So where did Mary's life go wrong?

After all, her upbringing was in a stable, loving and supportive home. Her father was a good provider and was always there for his family. Her brothers, well, let's just say a girl growing up with two strong-headed young men grows up to be a pretty resilient person herself.

Other than the typical sibling rivalry between brother and sister, the relationship between the Gretsis children was nothing out of the ordinary.

No!

Things went astray later in life. Mary was destined to wed young and have a child soon after. Mothering a child suited Mary. Nothing could have made her happier except for the fact she longed for her husband Charlie to be by her side. Charlie had other ideas and left for the gas fields.

A young man with a wife and child. Something snapped within him and with no real family of his own to turn to, he turned to the solitude of working in the outback.

Maybe Mary could have understood if he had taken the time to explain his feelings. But she was left all alone without a word being spoken.

One day her husband was there, the next he never came home. Mary knew he was alive. That was all. It was like he had fallen off the Earth with nowhere to be seen.

And with that, Mary fell into despair and misery.

Post–natal depression. It's what the specialist called it.

In the thick of it, Pam always put up a brave front. Pam held it all together even if those around her were falling apart. And regardless of the situation and the circumstances, Pam was always there for her little Tony even if Mary could not be.

Mary rode her highs and lows and Pam would be in the background to comfort and support. It must have been trying for her mum, not to mention the rest of her family. Two years on an emotional rollercoaster. But they all got through.

A morning Mary, and for that fact Pam, would never forget. A turning point in Mary came with the celebration of Tony's second birthday party. The planning of this little milestone event seem to bring a big part of the old Mary back. Everyone in the family noticed the change.

Mary still had her moments, but this event had her make a major leap towards returning to her former self.

Soon after, Charlie returned to seek his former wife. He wanted his family back. Those feelings again.

It was hard for Mary to take. It couldn't be easy dealing with a husband who had returned after a long and mysterious absence. Mary had a lot to consider and in doing so, she unintentionally put her family through hell, once again.

But when everyone was wanting no part of it, Pam chose to give the benefit of the doubt. It couldn't have been easy for her. After all, the possibility of Charlie abandoning his family again and Mary falling into another digressional state was very real.

Mary was willing to take the chance and Pam was there in the background waiting should it fall apart.

It shouldn't be like that, but it was.

Only for a short time. In the next few years, Charlie proved his dedication to his family and the Gretsis household never spoke of Charlie's earlier disappearance ever again. To this day, their son Tony never knew about his father's wayward ways.

All was great until Mary's surprise birthday celebration went horribly wrong.

Over a long weekend, Charlie and Mary went on a short getaway in a winery region close to home. A small time away wining and dining and spending some one on one time together.

A motor vehicle accident claimed Charlie's life on impact, but allowed Mary to survive for a short time afterwards until a stray clot to the heart claimed her life as well.

Mary could not imagine what her family went through, what her mother endured. The torture must have been unimaginable.

To put Mary on a hospital bed and to show small steps toward healing and recovery. To give a grieving family belief and offer some hope toward a recovery.

The whole Gretsis clan was there watching and praying their daughter, sister and mother would make it through some terrible injuries.

But it was not meant to be. And then just like that, suddenly it was all taken away.

Mary's death was quick.

And with her husband by her side, they got to spend their spiritual lives together until heaven had other plans for them.

But it didn't stop there.

Pam succumbed to a heart attack that took her quickly and Mary and Charlie would be there to greet their loving mother in the afterlife.

Pam's transition into heaven was difficult, however having Mary there made it easier.

Heaven had a mission for Charlie and Mary. Two special children in Germany would now have their own special guardian spirits. It was Charlie and Mary who followed these children. There was a task to be undertaken and Charlie and Mary would, for a better term, use the children until such time as they had no further use for them. Only then would they and could they return to heaven.

After a long absence, and in the afterlife, Mary was reunited with her mother.

Those were the times back then and how the times had changed now.

Heaven was now in trouble, taken over by demons and devil below.

Times were disruptive and everyone had their job in the battle of good versus evil.

Mary and Charlie came to a stop, looking ahead at the familiar face.

There was Pam in the distance, counselling with her words of support.

Close to a thousand children. These spirits had died young. They were all aged around their ten years before passing on and their spirits were relatively fresh to the heavens.

Instead of a peaceful afterlife, they were in the middle of a spiritual war. Pam's comforting words helped settle their troubled souls.

Charlie and Mary watched and waited.

"Charlie, I don't know how I am going to do it. Mum's been through too much already."

"I know it's not easy, love. Explain to your mother why. She has been in heaven for some time now. She will come to see the importance, I am sure of it."

Mary nodded, her face frowning and her soul riddled with sadness.

Soon after Pam finished with her group discussion. The children dispersed and were back in the arms of their respective family spirits and souls.

"Go on, love. There's no use putting it off." Charlie affectionately rubbed Mary's back and with a gentle push, persuaded her to go forth.

Mary only took a few steps before she caught the attention of her mother. Pam immediately waved and smiled, beaming from ear to ear. This did not make the task ahead any easier.

Pam made her way toward her daughter. Mary slowed her pace. Better she take a moment to prepare for the announcement she had been dreading.

Mary could never hide anything from her mother.

"What's wrong, dear?" asked Pam.

"Oh, Mum," Mary paused for a moment longer.

"What is it?" Pam asked again.

Mary could now see she had her mother a little worried as well. There was no point in delaying any further.

"Let's sit, Mum. Times like these are never easy and you are probably not going to like what I have to say."

Pam's normal bright and radiant face dulled to the paleness of a flu victim, her hands a little shaky as she made herself comfortable on heaven's floor.

"Mum. There was an incident that occurred when Sebastian was chasing down the boys in the streets of Germany. As you know, he left a trail of destruction. Some good people lost their lives so Sebastian could wander the streets in disguise. So that Sebastian could use their human form as transport."

"I know, dear. I met a few of them. I still see the poor preacher man from time to time. What a horrible way to pass. I have spent so much time with him and still do. He's better now, but it has affected him. He will carry this burden for the rest of his existence, but at least he is able to cope now."

"You have done such a wonderful job with him, Mum. Everyone can see it and this is why I know you will understand when I say Charlie and I are needed again. We are going to Earth to help with a troubled soul."

"Another big secret mission," Pam batted back, a hint of sarcasm in her voice.

"No, Mum. This time we can tell you. There was a young German lady Sebastian had come across, a middle aged lady. She had problems, Mum. You met her. She came to you with all sorts of troubles."

"I remember. She was very emotional. Extremely agitated. Unusual!" replied Pam.

"There's more to it, Mum. I hate to use the term, but she was kind of weird. Not all there if you know what I mean. But for where she lived, the locals knew her. She wandered the streets in the morning talking to herself. She lived in her own little delusional world. But she was harmless, Mum. Wouldn't hurt a fly. Everyone in the area got used to her. Let her do her bit. As crazy as she was, she was harmless."

Mary looked around to some of the ten year olds that were lingering in the near distance. She initiated her next discussion looking away to a few young spirits.

"You have experienced firsthand how a transition into heaven may not always go as smoothly as one would like."

Mary then turned to face her mother. "That's for everyday normal humans, but understandably this poor soul came to us with a troubled mind, combined with a horrific devilish encounter with Sebastian. This was simply a recipe for disaster," added Mary.

"We couldn't do anything with her. The angels sent her back down to live her life again in the hope rehabilitation could help," said Pam.

"Well it hasn't, Mum. There is something that has gone terribly wrong. We don't know what, but we are being sent to help and to do what we can. This deeply troubled soul needs our guidance. It needs our intervention so when her time comes again, she may return to heaven and warm to its glory and love instead of resisting it and despising it as she first did."

At this point Charlie joined in on the group. The only thing left to do was say their goodbyes. And this time, Pam whole heartedly understood.

As for the young, troubled girl who lived on Earth, who knew what results eventuate when you mix a soul that lived a previous life disturbed and troubled.

A soul which never had the opportunity to heal and re-establish normality in the afterlife.

A soul which had been violated by one as demonic and as evil as Sebastian.

This would be an unfortunate set of circumstances to inherit, but this unfortunate human was now living on Earth with a soul that had not been given its chance to be fully recycled.

The normal heavenly process of rehabilitation had been short changed and there would be unfinished business to attend to before this soul could return to heaven.

Heavenly intervention was on its way, but now the question had to be asked.

What price would Mary and Charlie now pay for their actions?

Chapter Ten
Johnny's Church

The church had been handed over to Johnny. Its preacher of many years, aged and in ill health, was unable to continue and so retired his position.

One month in and the young preacher was ecstatic. This was Johnny's congregation. Their souls were in his hands.

And to commemorate the new pastor, a large, hexagonally silver spire had replaced the old one. A single white crucifix housed securely at its top.

He looked the part, wearing his neatly pressed, all black cassock. It had thirty three buttons running from his neckline to lower abdomen. The number of buttons was symbolic of Christ's thirty three years on Earth.

The garment hung down on him like a long dress. The religious attire not complete without the white clerical neck collar.

The service finished and the people were long gone.

Johnny was pleased with his preaching of today and judging by the comments he got from the attendance, they were, too.

The front altar, a large stone bench—large enough to seat twelve but this was not a dining table.

Johnny tidied up in preparation for the next service. Everything had been removed from the bench top. He placed the bright white cloth, more than enough to cover the bench. Each side, draping down with a red crucifix stitched into its face. Johnny took a little time to ensure all crosses centred themselves. A little tug here and there and the Christian table cloth cover was perfectly positioned.

The young preacher picked up and placed his empty sacramental wine cup to one side of the bench, then his holy bible to centre position with a statue of Christ at the other end.

The inspiring statue stood a little over one and half feet. All white and marble, it showed Christ standing as the scriptures had described him, beckoning to the people with open arms in the most pleasant manner as if saying "Come unto me."

The young preacher positioned the statue just right and then walked around and stepped back into the church pews. He took a final look at the front of the altar as if he were seated as one of the congregation.

Picture perfect!

Just then a young lady walked into the church. She was probably not much older than Johnny.

She looked tired, worn out.

"Can I help you?" asked Johnny.

"Yes, Father. We have just moved into the area and wanted to introduce ourselves to the local church."

"That's very kind of you, but the Sunday service is over. You are most welcome to attend. We have," Johnny was interrupted as he was about to highlight the various starting times.

"Father, please forgive my directness, but may I ask a favour. Can you please bless our home? We have come seeking a fresh start and it would mean so much to me if you could bless our house."

This lady put out the request as if time was of the essence. There was something more to this, but Johnny didn't persist with the matter, instead they introduced themselves.

A single mother, her name was Angela.

Unlike her namesake, this lady was no angel, but a human servant of the one that now ruled the heavens.

They set a date for the end of the week.

Angela was grateful and grabbed the hand of the pastor and kissed it before bowing, doing her cross and exiting the church.

She played the part of a God-loving Christian well.

Johnny watched her leave and then turned to walk into his office situated at the rear of the church.

Way above in the grounds of heaven, the devil was working hard to influence some of Earth's weather. In particular, he wanted to send his young human preacher enemy a little present.

The devil used his powers to persuade Mother Nature to bring forth a gusty wind.

Johnny was seated at his desk, finalising some notes. He could hear the breeze gather momentum. With every second it got louder and louder, blowing for longer and longer.

It howled like a wolf as if it were wounded and crying for help.

This time the airflow caught Johnny's attention. The young man stopped what he was doing, looked up and listened.

It blew with incredible strength and sounded like it had enveloped the entire church, every bit of wall and window creaking from the strain.

The sounds came in from all around.

Johnny listened. It was getting louder, close to unbearable.

The windy cries were eerie and it seemed as though the walls of this old church were struggling. The strains of the structure were creaking inside almost as loud as the outside wind.

Internally and externally, combined, the noises were uncomfortably loud.

This went on for a few more seconds until suddenly, there was a big crash. The sound clearly came from beyond the walls of the church, outside and nearby.

Instantly, Johnny jumped up out of his seat and dashed out the backdoor. Soon he was face to face with the windstorm.

He wanted to run, but the best he could do looked more like a drunken stagger. The harder Johnny ran, the more Mother Nature pushed back. This continued until he made his way to the front grounds.

Just then, the hurricane-like gale dwindled down to a moderate breeze.

The damage was evident. The Lord's house was no match for the devil's gift. Mother Nature's raging wind had torn the newly placed, six hundred kilogram spire from its placing. The twisted ten metre stainless steel structure lay on the ground as a small crowd gathered around.

"Father, are you okay?" asked a middle aged man.

"I'm fine. Thankfully no one was hurt."

Johnny looked up, assessing the damage. The middle aged man was near his side.

"You are lucky, Father. Had it blown the other way, your roof would not have stood a chance. The damage would have been quite costly."

Johnny's face went from worried to relieved. In times of crisis, his job was to hold it together. Whilst this strange phenomenon had him shaky on the inside, he would not allow his true feelings to surface. His priority was for his people.

"It's nothing the insurance companies can't take care of," Johnny added.

The damage slowly drew a crowd and the banter grew amongst them, however the preacher and his people remained calm and collected.

This ordeal, however, was not over.

Another parting gift from the one they call Lucifer.

Inside the church, the statue of Christ wobbled, tipping side to side and leaning a little more than it did the time before.

On its fifth cycle, it toppled over, crashing to the ground; only this time there was no one around to hear it.

The all-white marble statue lay on the floor broken into six pieces whilst way up in heaven's grounds, the devil smirked at the thought of such a good day's work.

Chapter Eleven
A Park Bench

Johnny sat at his church office desk, located at the back, away from those distracting traffic noises.

However, all was not quiet. Work had begun on the repair of the steeple and at times, the men at work and their noisy tools made it hard to concentrate.

But life goes on and there was paperwork that needed to be completed. About another hour's work and he would be caught up.

The desk was empty except for the paperwork and a plain black sunglass case.

Johnny stopped and picked up the case.

He opened it to admire the sunglasses cushioned neatly inside. The plain black frame was stylish enough with the bridge of the sunglasses marked with a gold emblem resembling a king's crown. The crown was leaning to one side much like the tilt given to letters in italics. The lenses were tinted and looked untouched. They appeared expensive and in excellent condition, but then again, Johnny was no expert on sunglasses, nor did he recognise the brand symbol.

Johnny put down the case to the front of him, but out of the way of his spread out sheets of paper. He kept the case lid opened and stopped for a few seconds more to admire the gift he was going to give to his friend for his twenty fifth birthday.

The young priest had given up his materialistic side. Gifts and presents were not something Johnny would normally do. It came with the job of being one of God's dedicated servants.

The gift situation was well understood by all his family and friends.

Yet sometimes there were exceptions to the rule and one would be made today.

Well sort of.

Johnny would have wished his friend well with no gift to give. He would have stuck to his personal life values of not giving of things that were materialistic.

This gift was not purchased, but was in the church's lost and found for many months. No-one had laid claim to them and Johnny could see no harm in giving it to his closest friend.

Johnny knew the birthday boy well enough to know he would not be expecting anything other than a congratulatory birthday handshake.

Johnny was looking forward to surprising him the next time they met, but for now, it was back to the paperwork.

~ * ~

It was 1991 and Tony was near to closing his twenty fifth year. There was something Tony needed to find out. Tony never knew, but he was about to discover a hidden family secret.

A promise had been made between the uncles and the grandfather to keep it secret. On Tony's twenty fifth birthday, the time had come to tell him.

This was all about Tony's father and how the family home came to be.

He sat at the table with his grandfather directly in front of him. His uncles Jack and Chris were to his sides. They didn't do much other than add a little word or two every now and then.

Arthur took the lead.

His grandfather must have been nervous because the stories of his father's history seem to come out in one continuous sentence.

Tony sat there all quiet-like. The tale had begun and he did not take well to the news. After all, his father was perfect in his eyes. When he was alive, he lived for his family. There was nothing he wouldn't do for his son or his wife. That's how Tony remembered his long deceased father.

But now, Tony had to hear that life wasn't so grand. That for a small time in his infant life, his father had abandoned his family. He left Mary all alone to deal with her one and only son.

"Your mother didn't cope all too well. We all pitched in and did our bit," Arthur added.

Tony sensed there was more to this, but his grandfather was quick to move on from the topic.

He now talked about how Tony's father fought to win his family back. Tony listened, but he couldn't get past the fatherly abandonment. What was so bad that it drove a father to leave his family unexpectedly and why would he not make any sort of contact? Why would he leave his mother to suffer like he had done?

Tony listened some more as his grandfather spoke about Charlie and the sacrifice he made to win back Mary. This all tied into how the family home came to be purchased.

The family put forth their views on the risk Mary was taking to bring Charlie back into her life. The home was given to Mary unconditionally by Charlie. If he was to leave again, at least Mary and Tony wouldn't have to worry about somewhere to live. This was Charlie's guarantee.

Charlie won over Mary and with that came Tony. Yet, like every soul in the world, we come packaged with relatives, history and memories.

Charlie had to also win back his dignity and respect from brothers-in-law, father-in-law and a mother-in-law. He had to prove his worth to being an extended and loving member of the Gretsis family again.

Tony kept his mouth shut tight. He dare not speak as speaking could quickly turn into yelling. This was not easy to take.

He would if he could.

First he'd yell at his grandfather for keeping such important information locked away from him for all these years. Then he'd scream, letting loose the built up frustration within him. Explode violently like a volcano eruption. This was how Tony would have liked to have done it but all this young man could manage was a polite, "Excuse me, I need some time to myself."

Tony walked out of the room, ensuring no eye contact was made with any member of his family.

He didn't want to face them.

He found some privacy; made a quick phone call to Johnny.

"Johnny!" Tony blurted over the phone.

Tony's friend sensed the urgency straight away. "What's wrong?" Johnny replied.

"I really can't speak. Not here, not now. Can you meet me at the park? You know the spot," Tony stated.

"Are you okay?" Johnny asked again, but his friend cut the conversation to a blunt question.

"Can you meet with me or not?" Tony demanded.

"Okay, okay. Just take it easy. Give me twenty or thirty minutes to finish off and I'll see you there."

"Thanks." Tony's reply finished with a quick hanging up of the phone.

Tony couldn't get out of the house fast enough. Soon after, Tony was there, sitting at one of the many park benches in one of the city's major parklands. This was a place Johnny and Tony would visit many a time as children. Back then a nice long walk would get them there, but today, Tony drove his second hand, four cylinder Mazda, parking its faded yellow body in one of the parking lanes on the northern end and walking a few minutes to get to the designated meeting place.

He sought comfort and perhaps Johnny could help him see the positive in this big negative. Until Johnny arrived, Tony had little choice but to dwell on this all on his own.

Phase one of the process had passed. The short drive to the park with several punches on the steering wheel and grunts and screams of resentment had already taken place in the privacy of the inside of his car.

Perhaps not the best way to drive a car, but better this be done in private and not in a public parkland.

Now sitting on a park bench, Tony wondered as to why it took so long to tell him. Something about the family agreeing to speak on his twenty fifth birthday. He couldn't understand why the importance of this particular age.

Why twenty five, why not twenty one or nineteen?

How ridiculous, Tony thought.

Whatever happened to good old common sense? Whatever happened to the open and honest policy that supposedly existed after his grandmother's death?

Arthur insisted the males of the family come together for a regular weekend luncheon where Jack, Arthur, Chris and Tony could take the time to be involved in everyone's lives.

What a joke. For the moment, he never wanted to go to another one of his grandfather's barbeque luncheons ever again.

The anger subsided just a little. Then Tony thought back.

The emotions of having to live through the days and months shortly after his parents' deaths rushed back through his memory banks with a vengeance.

The hurt inside was overwhelming.

An inconspicuous wipe or two with his index finger and the few tears that had formed were quickly gone without a trace. No person playing in the parkland had noticed, Tony made sure of that.

When his mother and father died, Tony would have gladly sold the home for nothing. Given it away if it could take the hurtful feelings away that went with the death of his parents. Unfortunately life was not that simple and Tony was left to grieve for the loss of his mother and father and to deal with the memories that flooded his mind every time he set foot in his family home.

Stepping into his house was unbearable, so Tony's grandparents took over. Emptied the home, kept what had to be kept and gave away the rest. Rented it out and the money was put aside for Tony's future.

Tony was too young to comprehend or perhaps not. If someone had taken the time back then to explain the circumstances surrounding the family inheritance then maybe he might have taken more interest in the situation at hand.

Instead he kept his distance.

Maybe he was partly to blame for the lateness of the news.

Absence of information. It was not his fault, it was theirs. How could he have known?

The opportunity to forgive the male members of Tony's family presented itself and then passed by just as quickly. They were not going to get off that easy!

There was indeed a close and personal history to his family home.

He now wondered at the complexities which must have occurred when his dad returned from working in the gas fields in middle outback Australia. What his father must have gone through to re-establish the love and trust of his wife, Mary. Winning the rest of the family over couldn't have been easy either.

In all this time, Tony looked down. His fists were loosely clenched as he stared at the path below.

All these thoughts ran through his head.

He lifted his head and checked for his friend, but Johnny had not arrived.

Tony then turned to face the open greenery before him. A large, open, grassed area with trees bordering the circumference providing shade for picnicking families.

Low cut grass, as large as three football ovals. Swings and slides, large trees and miscellaneous playthings spread out on the outer edges for young and old to enjoy.

A light breeze blowing with tree branches gently swaying to and fro. A picture perfect day of gentle warmth with intermittent whispers of fresh cool winds.

A family caught his attention. They were maybe a little over one hundred feet to the front and slightly off to the right hand side of where he sat.

For the first time, Tony sat back and looked upwardly. He twisted his body slightly to the right so he could look directly at them.

A grandfather type figure with an adult male cooked on their portable barbeque whilst two mothers and an elderly lady oversaw their young boys kick a miniature soccer ball.

It was hard to say if the two mothers were related, however the older lady had very similar facial features to one of the mothers.

Either way, Tony watched as a grandmother held onto one of the boys' hands as he kicked the ball. Uncoordinated, but he hit the ball with a solid right foot swing. One of the mothers then had a pretend race with the other young boy, edging him on to get to the ball first.

They played a scrappy game of childish soccer. The mothers ran and laughed at their efforts. The grandmother stood on the sidelines coaxing what looked like her grandson. The young boys played against each other, their movements highly uncoordinated, but their sporting egos extremely competitive.

Tony watched on. There were no goals. Just kicks and dribbles and chases and more kicks with more laughter and a lot of fun.

Tony sat back in his park bench chair. This time he was more attentive and more alert. He watched the antics of the young boys with their mothers and grandmother play on for a little longer.

The similarities were uncanny. It was like looking into a mirror of family moments long passed.

Family friends perhaps or blood relatives, it didn't matter.

These two young boys had a bond and good luck to them if their friendship ended up half of what Tony and Johnny shared.

A loving and gentle grandmother on the sidelines ready to support in times of needs. It reminded him of his relationship with Pam, his now deceased grandmother.

A smile surfaced on Tony's face as he looked on and heard the father and grandfatherly figure call the family in to enjoy some freshly cooked barbeque meats and homemade salads.

The grandfather dished his meats onto the children's plate. One of the young boys walked away from the portable barbeque, but not before he got a kiss on the top of his head from a loving grandfather.

It suddenly hit Tony. As if an invisible hand had slapped him in the face and said, "Wake up to the truth."

Had Tony missed the point about this situation?

Tony loved his grandfather and somewhere in the last hour or so, this had been forgotten.

His grandfather was there when times were tough. He was the rock of foundation when Tony had to contend with the deaths in the family.

The emotions and anguish quickly disappeared.

The past was what it was and with calmness came the clarity. Arthur would never do anything to upset his grandson. Not intentionally anyway.

How negative emotions tarnish the ability to see the true intent.

They loved each other too much to allow something like this to get in the middle of a special relationship. How could Tony have thought such ill thoughts about his family? They were only protecting his interests.

This was the only conclusion to draw from the news and events of today.

Tony turned his head and saw Johnny approaching. He was dressed casually; jeans, black T-shirt and a lightweight denim jacket.

"Sorry. I got delayed. You sounded upset. What's going on?" blurted Johnny.

Tony smiled as he got up and patted the back of his long-time friend.

"Let's go get a coffee."

The phone call Tony had made to Johnny was filled with heated emotion and yet this parkland greeting was quite the opposite. Nothing other than calm and collected.

At a nearby café, Tony explained his understandable, but silly reaction over a hot coffee. Johnny also saw both sides of the equation. This came down to nothing other than a loving family, wanting to protect a young man from finding out the hurtful truth.

At the conclusion of their friendly get together, Johnny surprised his friend with his special little birthday gift.

Tony loved the sunglasses. It was indeed a wonderful birthday surprise.

It had been a long day of emotional highs and lows, but in the end, all that mattered was all had been forgiven.

Chapter Twelve
Angela and Allie

In a world where right and wrong are not absolute, where shades of grey exist in almost every foreseeable situation, then evil isn't just avoidable—it's necessary.

~ * ~

Angela had worked hard to present a respectable home for the coming priestly visit. In a few more hours Father Johnny would be there to bless her home.

Angela put away her vacuum cleaner and walked back into the main dining room. She caught the eye of her seven year old daughter, Allie, who was seated on the black sofa recliner. Angela let out a sinister giggle as she threw her head back ever so slightly, still maintaining eye contact with Allie. Her evil sound of laughter filled the room. Both mother and daughter knew what was about to happen.

Angela watched Allie put aside her playthings and then she held out her hand. Allie put her hand in her mother's gentle grip.

In the room, the spirits of Mary and Charlie kept a close watch.

"There she is," stated Mary, as she pointed her finger to Allie. "She's the one Mum was dealing with back in heaven. That German lady who was all disturbed and anguished. Her disturbed soul has returned to Earth and is in that body."

"Those souls are evil. My very being feels like there are hundreds of spiders crawling inside of me. This feels so very wrong," added Charlie.

"I know. I feel the same, but we must trust in the Angels and their instructions. We need to keep an eye on these two."

Hand in hand, Angela led Allie to the room door. A room she kept locked at all times. Her daughter was standing beside her as she inserted the key. The action was a little stiff and took a little bit of jiggling before she turned the lock action. She left the key in the keyhole, opened the door and with the gentle persuasion of her hand on her daughter's back, let Allie enter first.

Unbeknown to the women of this evil household, the spirits of Charlie and Mary were also close by.

This room had originally been designed as a bedroom. It was on the small side of size but there was certainly enough space for a single bed and one or two furniture pieces.

Angela, Allie and the uninvited spiritual guests all walked into their room of worship.

This room was no bedroom.

Very much alarmed, Mary spoke, "My God, Charlie, what have we walked into?"

It was completely empty aside from the four large grey cushions set down on the wooded floor below. But it was what else Mary saw of the room that concerned her.

Two side walls painted in black. Symbols of evil painted on them.

In a dark red, a large pentacle, a five sided star sitting within a circle on one side and on the opposite black wall, the demon's number of six, six, six painted in a triangular fashion with the tails of the numbers all pointed to the centre. The sixes stretched out to the entire length and width of the wall.

Adjacent to the black were walls of red. This shade of red was different to that of the painted symbols; richer and brighter in colour, like the colour of oxygenated blood. The red walls were unmarked except for one solitary picture which hung on the back wall.

The portrait caught Mary's attention for the moment. How could you miss it, for it was large enough, measuring three feet wide and five feet long? The picture was of the master himself. The demonic leader they call Lucifer, depicted with reddish skin, horns and hoofed feet. His face, intensely stared back with blank white eyeballs and a cheeky smirk.

At first glance, Mary thought nothing of the black background of the portrait but upon closer inspection, this was no background colour, but black and majestic wings. The blackness filled the backdrop of the picture, Lucifer's wings made out with bony articulations and segmented leathery textures, similar to the wings of a bat, only in this case, the size of the wings were blown largely out of proportion, so much so that the artist of this picture could not fit them onto his canvas.

This wasn't what all would call an accurate representation of Lucifer, but it was close enough and it certainly made the point. Everything done in this room was only for sinister intent.

Mary and Charlie oversaw Angela and Allie as they made themselves comfortable on the cushions below and within seconds of doing so, began their chants and devilish screams. Their seated bodies were now moving in small revolutions. They moved as they sung their hellish chants to their master.

A room so well insulated, the women of this household yelled out their devilish prayers, without a single note reaching the outside for others to hear. Very quickly, the room filled with screams and yells gradually getting louder and louder.

Allie covered her ears trying to dampen the deafening sounds that echoed within. This did not stop her as she continued to yell out her evil chants alongside her mother, both of them being as loud as they possibly could.

Their tongues wiggled from side to side as they let their hellish-ridden souls surface to freely express their love for all that was evil. They expressed their gratitude with high shrieks and blood curdling screams. Mother and daughter bonded together by a love for Lucifer and his army of evildoers.

In the spiritual plane, Mary turned to Charlie.

"Honey, this is out of our depth. I know we are here to observe, but I really think we need the help of an archangel."

Mary hugged her husband. She knew he would understand.

"I'll be right back." After a parting kiss on the cheek, Mary disappeared out of view, leaving Charlie to monitor and observe.

~ * ~

In another section of the city of Adelaide, Tony parked his car on a dirt road not all that far from the water's edge.

It was an easy enough and out of the way spot to get to, a nearby port only a thirty or so minute drive from the family home. With his tackle box and fishing rod in one hand and his birthday present sunglasses on, he used his free hand to help him manoeuvre down the large rocky embankment. There was no danger here as long as he didn't rush and watched his step.

Tony had been here many a time before. He lowered himself onto the rocky pathway with no trouble.

This was saltwater marshland, dominated mainly by woody trees set in the water close to the shoreline. There was the occasional grass saltwater bush and plenty of small rocks, but for most of the way, the ground was free from the smaller variety of vegetation.

Tony's thick soled camping boots sunk only a fraction with each step. The closer he got to the shoreline, the little more they sunk. Tony knew better; when he found himself sinking to the material line of his shoes, then that was as close as he got to the water's edge.

A large rock ideal for a makeshift seat. An opening in the woody trees, an area large enough to fish without the worry of a snagged or entangled fishing line.

Soon, his line was in and Tony was looking across to the other side of the salt water wetland.

The sun's glare reflected off the slow moving tide, but his new sunglasses would deal with that concern.

There were two males on the other side of the saltwater marshland, the distance between them enough to not bother Tony and his day of solitary fishing.

Tony wiggled around, making himself a little more comfortable on his rocky seat. He then leant back a little and looked up as he continued to watch the tip of his fishing rod for that all-inspiring first bite.

Chapter Thirteen
If Only He Knew

Charlie, in the spiritual plane, was doing everything possible to deter this young man from entering a house of evil. He was communicating directly with the soul of a holy man, waving his arms like a crazed lunatic.

For some unknown reason, Charlie thought the more vigorous the movement, the more likely something may get through from the spiritual plane to the physical part of Johnny.

Johnny stopped.

An involuntary shiver ran through his body.

He was at the doorstep of Angela's house.

Johnny paused for a moment longer.

If only he knew...

Charlie did get through, but he had only postponed the inevitable for a handful of seconds. The priest dismissed any strange, spiritual borne sensations and rang the doorbell only to be greeted by Angela soon after.

"Hello, Father. Please come in."

With a courteous smile, Johnny was led to the kitchen of this evil household.

"Coffee? Tea?"

"A tea would be lovely," replied Johnny. "White and no sugar please."

"Sweet enough, are we?" replied Angela.

Johnny would have answered the corny remark with some quick witted light humour but was saved by the entrance of Allie. "And who is this?" asked Johnny.

"Allie, say hello to the Father," asked Angela of her daughter.

The reply was shy-like, a soft hello came out of her sweet voice box and then Allie quickly ran to the solitude of another room.

"Forgive her, Father. It's not been an easy time for us. I guess Allie is a bit uncomfortable around strangers."

"As it should be. Think nothing of it," replied Johnny.

The time had come to sit and drink their hot beverages. Johnny took a moment to talk with Angela. He wanted to help, but before he could help, he had to understand.

It was time to get to know each other a little better.

If only he knew...

Watching from the spiritual plane, Charlie had taken an interest in Allie's quick departure. Charlie could appreciate why Johnny might have thought nothing of it.

And how could Charlie warn Johnny about the events that he had come to witness only earlier today.

He wanted Johnny to follow Allie, but there was no way he knew of to communicate the dangers of this situation and so for the time being, he had given up on trying.

All he could do was observe and monitor from his spiritual world.

Alas, the sudden departure of this young child was not given a second thought by the adults in the room.

Charlie, however, perceived the moment with a bit more caution.

Allie was on her way to the room of worship.

Charlie was close behind.

The key was sticking out of the keyhole and the door had remained closed, but unlocked from the mother and daughter chanting session earlier today.

The young girl opened the entrance to the room, peeking her head in, if only for a few extended seconds.

Charlie remained outside.

When her young face returned from around the door, she stopped and stood still.

She shut her eyelids so tight, ensuring that no speckle of daylight would get through. She then clenched her tiny fists and tensed the rest of her body, as if she was desperately wishing for something to happen.

A little bit of time passed.

Charlie watched on.

Her young body trembled with miniature shakes as every muscle went stiff. Her shoulders were up, her forehead wrinkled; her back arched a little, her young muscles flexed.

This position held for a couple of minutes longer.

And then, the transformation was sudden.

Completely relaxed.

Her eyelids shut, but not as tight as before.

Her body showed the signs of being more soft and feminine. Her shoulders had dropped her posture much more elegant and upright, her face displayed the gentleness and sweetness typical of a young lady.

Before her eyes were to open again, a smile would emerge and remain on her pretty young face. It could have been seen as cute and innocent, but Charlie knew better.

The smile stayed, beaming from ear to ear.

Suddenly, she opened her eyes as wide as they could go.

In the initial moment, it was as if she were glaring straight into Charlie's eyes and Charlie's into hers.

A stare for only a few long seconds.

The young girl then broke her eye contact and turned to lock the door. As young as she might have been, she at least had the common sense to understand this was no room for any strangers to witness, particularly a visiting priest.

As Allie took the key to put it securely away in her mother's bedroom, Charlie's spirit stood outside the doorway.

Charlie didn't know what to think.

Surely, she couldn't have seen him standing there.

He chose to stay and not follow Allie.

If only he knew!

Chapter Fourteen
Unfinished Business

He watched Allie disappear into her mother's bedroom.

Charlie stood there all silent and perplexed.

After a short moment, Charlie turned to face the doorway. He sensed it, but could not know for certain. There was something more to this room of worship.

The door may have been locked, but spiritual beings were not limited by the physical and biological laws of the Earth.

Charlie stepped through the doorway as if it were a hanging curtain. A little resistance and with a few steps he had passed through.

His eyes widened immediately. What he saw shocked him instantly.

Face to face with two demonic soldiers. He and them in a room designed for devilish worship.

They appeared as surprised as he, but before Charlie could respond, one of the demonic warriors had already reacted to the unannounced visit, moving in quickly to restrain Charlie. The demonic warrior had his evil forearm across Charlie's throat in next to no time, holding him from behind.

Charlie did not resist. He thought he may have had the strength to shake off one demonic beast, but to take on two was a near impossibility.

These were warrior class demons; he was but a simple soul. Charlie did not resist his captors and as frightened as he was on the inside, his outwardly glare of hatred of all things demonic would hide his inwardly feelings.

The second soldier walked towards him.

His skin charred and singed and eyes large, black and sunken.

These demons were as ugly as they were evil.

The soldier walked up to Charlie and snarled. His teeth rotten and jagged.

Charlie knew he was in trouble and there was absolutely nothing he could do about it.

Charlie feared for his existence. So he did the only thing he could do for now, his thoughts drifting as he silently prayed that Mary return with the archangel before it was too late.

~ * ~

Back on the water's edge, Tony sat on his rock, baiting up his hook. He had caught himself three medium sized whiting and was eager to get his fourth.

He cast the line back into the saltwater aiming for the spot that had brought him his third catch for the afternoon.

'Couldn't get much closer,' he thought to himself as he watched the sinker hit and plop into the water.

There was a nibble on the rod almost instantly, but the fish had not hooked itself. Tony waited for that second bite, at the ready to jerk his rod and hook his fourth.

Suddenly, Tony's vision went a bit hazy. He lowered his rod, removed his sunglasses and rubbed his eyes.

Tony was not ill, feverish or dizzy and yet his eyes had lost their ability to focus, if only for the moment.

He removed his glasses and soon after, re-looked across the water. His vision was clear and focussed. He could see the people across the saltwater, fishing and moving about. He looked close by at the nearby marshland and the picture was as crisp and clear as the hand on the end of his arm.

Not giving it a second thought, he put his sunglasses back on and almost immediately, the landscape went hazy again.

Tony removed his sunglasses within a fraction of a second, rubbing his eyes for a second time. He then looked around again noting there was no issue with his vision.

He then inspected his new sunglasses, viewing them front and back. There was nothing notably different about the gift he had been given by his close friend. All appeared okay.

He put them back on his head and within seconds his vision of a saltwater body of water marshland disappeared completely out of view only to be replaced with visions of flame and fire.

His entire soul was now engaged in the hallucination before him. His peripheral vision now replaced with colours of burning reds, yellows and ambers. The flames remained like a frame around a photo. They burned with flame tips dancing left and right. Their tips reaching inwardly. Everything peripheral was nothing but flames whilst the middle of the vision remained black and blank.

Tony wasn't frightened, more so, hypnotised by the vision. He watched on as if he were watching a television up close. A television whose screen was blank and whose borders were a fiery rage.

Suddenly in his own little private movie picture viewing, the film-like images began to play. No sound, only visual.

There was his father struggling to get free of a monster.

But wait, there were two. One holding his father, the other about to approach him.

His father looked worried.

The second beast approached Charlie and clasped his face with his two demonic hands.

He put his face up to Charlie's, their respective noses only an inch apart.

In his trance-like state, Tony watched on. He wanted to help, but wouldn't know how.

Tony watched from his stationary position. If only he knew that he was watching actual time, watching real time demonic torture of the spiritual kind.

The vision closed in. All Tony could see was the head of the demon staring into the face of his father.

The demon's eyes focussed on the human spirit before him; he snarled. If Tony had sound, the tone of the demon would be low and deep, resonating like the sound of a downpour on a bituminous road. If Charlie had a heartbeat, it would be pounding at a million beats a minute.

Alas, none of these existed. Tony watched in silence as Charlie's face showed defeat mixed in with a bucket load of terror.

With silence and exhausted stares, simply put, Charlie feared for his spiritual existence.

The demonic soldier was now communicating with the core of Charlie's soul. Torturing it like a cat to a cornered mouse. The beast's face became more and more intense, its face trembled with incredible speed.

The vibrating demon's head blurred out of focus, moving only a little to the left and then a little to the right.

Back and forth, back and forth until Charlie's look of fear went to a look of nothing.

The demon stopped, removing his clasped hand from Charlie's face.

The sunglasses continued to be Tony's little private viewing screen, as if a camera was filming the whole event. The vision before Tony changed perspectives, this time focussing in on only the beast's face.

An evil smirk of sorts, the demon displaying his shark-like teeth again. Tony may have been paralysed for the moment, but the finale did not stop the goose bumps forming and the hairs on his arms standing erect.

The movie-like image then panned across to his dad. Charlie was standing there in a daze, unwilling to move.

Seconds later, Charlie collapsed as if every bit of strength in his legs had been taken away.

In the foetal position he lay.

Tony's private viewing suddenly came to an end and as soon as it did, Tony swiped the sunglasses off his head.

His heart now pounding, he stared at the sunglasses sitting in the wet sand.

The fishing was over.

Minutes later, his gear was packed and he was climbing the rocks to get to his car. He chucked everything in; he couldn't get away quick enough.

In the driver's seat, ready to start the car, he paused.

As concerning as it may have been, something about this strange vision appeared awfully familiar to him.

He got out of the car, navigated himself down the rocks and retrieved his sunglasses. He would not put them on his head but in his shirt pocket.

The surreal experience would have to be shared. Would Johnny believe him?

~ * ~

In the spiritual plane, Mary returned with Archangel Gabriel.

"Oh no!" she exclaimed. "What have they done to you?" Mary asked aloud as she rushed to her husband's aid and knelt beside his collapsed spiritual form.

Archangel Gabriel was aware of the signs of demonic attack.

"Come, Mary, we must get back immediately."

Gabriel picked up Charlie and the three would soon return to their homeland.

As Gabriel held Charlie, and with Mary at his side, the process of dematerialising had begun. In a few seconds, the three of them would be teleported to a plane of heaven where Charlie's injuries could be attended to.

~ * ~

Johnny was leaving while this spiritual dissipation was taking place, none the wiser after having blessed the house, completely oblivious to the evil that had just occurred a room away from where he had sat visiting with Angela.

Gabriel looked around at the evil room he was about to leave. It was the first time Gabriel was able to truly absorb all that was around him. As they began to phase out for their spiritual journey to up above, Gabriel would observe to see for the first time the concerning images of large demonic symbols and images on every wall of this room of worship.

The impressions left with the archangel needn't be explained.

Chapter Fifteen
Angel Zophiel and Madame Liz

In the heavenly plane, there was separation. A space between those who are good and those who are evil, up above, where angels wait and on the grounds below, where demon footprints flow.

For the time, there was silence.

There were no demonic snarls, no angelic screams. The odd demonic or spiritual conversation here and there, but mainly all activity had dulled to a complete standstill.

Demon was largely ignorant of the angelic hierarchy above.

Equally, angel and spirit had become accustomed to their new way of life. It had become routine by now, as they went about their day to day business, ignoring the invading terrors below.

Madame Liz wandered the upper grounds of heaven. Her psychic abilities had been bothering her.

Glimpses of visions puzzling her at first, but had, over time, come together like the putting together of a massive jigsaw puzzle. Her gift as a psychic medium on Earth continued to be with her in her spiritual passing.

With more pieces came a clearer message and with clarity came her search for a special angel.

Soon after, her voice across the heavenly land was heard by many. She broke the silence, screaming his name. She was determined and the need to meet with the Great Zophiel was urgent.

Immune to the attraction of everyone's attention, she ran toward the great angel with a sort of excited stride. As she drew closer, she struggled to maintain her eyes on the great glow emanating from this angelic being.

The brightness hurt her eyes. She did not look his way when she spoke to him, but she could see enough to know Zophiel was looking at her.

Her message was straight to the point.

"May we speak, Zophiel? Can we go somewhere private?"

Zophiel walked away from the immediate crowd and Madame Liz accompanied the angel. Until they were at his chosen destination, no further words had been spoken.

A little corner of Heaven, as private as one could get in the spiritual land, a few more steps and they would both be there.

"And what is it you seek?" asked Zophiel.

They stopped to observe all that was around, up and down.

"Look!" Madame Liz shifted her vision to the grounds below where demonic bodies littered the white billowy floor. Outside of the demonic vermin plastered from one end of heaven's ground to the other, this was also symbolic of heavenly defeat. She did not speak, but waited for the great angel to comment.

She didn't have to wait long.

"It worries me they are still here. It is not like heaven to be held to ransom by those from the dark." Zophiel stopped looking down and raised his head to meet with hers.

The glare from his face may have been brighter than any searchlight, but for the short amount of time that Liz could tolerate it, she stared directly into the angel's face.

It only lasted a handful of seconds and then Liz looked away. She tried not to, but it was hard not to rub her eyes.

His arms and hands, more fitting to a grizzly bear as opposed to a high ranking angel, were gently put around Liz's shoulders as he persuaded her to walk onwards.

The two continued to walk away from any prying ears.

Madame Liz was sympathetic. How could one not be!

For the first time in all of man's existence, heaven's homeland was in chaos. Invaded and occupied by demons all around. This could not be easy for any spiritual entity, especially not one as high in rank as Zophiel.

But whilst all around was doom and gloom, Madame Liz was almost excitable. "I think I have found the answer," she blurted.

"My dear spirit, answer to what?" replied Zophiel.

"This. All this!" Her hand went out pointing to the demonic invasion below.

Zophiel stopped and Liz reacted similarly.

"The devil is ruthless and has proved he will go to whatever extremes to make his mark. Anything he does, he does for his own selfish reasons. There is little consideration for those around him."

"This has always been his way," added Zophiel.

"Then I see it. I see what he wants more than anything in this world. I wasn't sure what it meant at first. I would see glimpses. Visions!"

Madame Liz stopped again, waving her hand at the grounds below.

"I am certain of it. He'd give this all up, if we could grant him his one desire."

"And what would that be?" asked Zophiel.

"To be human. To live on Earth as flesh and blood. To be born and to rule."

"Satan is indeed in the churches as prophesised," Zophiel mumbled these words under his breath.

"What?" asked Liz. She did not hear the words of the great Angel nor was she meant to. The words spoken were for his angelic ears only and so his reply to her question was a subtle shake of his head as if to say, 'Don't worry about it.'

After an uncomfortable and brief pause, Liz continued. "I have seen it," stated Liz.

Zophiel lifted his bear-like arm off her shoulder. Liz and Zophiel now walked separately but together.

"I can see the day where he no longer occupies the spiritual plane. This will leave his army leaderless and it will mark a turning point for heaven. We will all have our day."

Zophiel mumbled a response, similar to what he had done only moments before.

"And mankind will suffer for it!" The response was as silent as any whisper could be, but this time, Madame Liz heard.

Chapter Sixteen
The Devil You Know

The Tuesday morning wind howled at the all grey sky. An argument of sorts was only going to end with crashing thunder and bright streaks of lightning, but as of now, the low hanging clouds had not replied.

Tony was at the rear office of Johnny's church.

The wind continued to yell as if it were in anger, a grim sound creating a muffled backdrop for the conversation about to take place inside the church walls.

Tony looked at Johnny, his best friend on the opposite side of the pastor's table. Tony was seated leaning in towards the table top, Johnny's swivel chair at a slight angle, but also leaning in towards the friendly discussion.

They mirrored each other's body language to a tee.

A stationary cup filled with half a dozen assorted coloured pens and a few lead pencils sat to the right of the table. Neatly sorted in front of them was a small pile of papers and to the left hand corner of the desk was a pair of birthday present sunglasses.

At this moment, Johnny was more interested in observing the sunglasses.

"You still don't believe me, do you?" asked Tony.

Johnny maintained a casual stare at the glasses. He raised his elbow to the table and rested his chin in the palm of his hand. The item hadn't moved since Tony returned them to him after his demonic visions. Johnny kept his stare to the corner of the desk, wondering how he best reply to his friends question.

Under normal circumstances, this wasn't a difficult question to answer. Why would one believe a story about putting sunglasses on and suddenly the water in which you are fishing looks more like flame and fire? Why would one believe a pair of black sunglasses would allow you the ability to see demons and spirits? Anyone else would have scoffed at the idea, but not Johnny.

The concern was raised back then and Johnny just listened. Nothing more was said and it had not been spoken about at any length or detail until now.

A month passed since Tony's fishing adventure and if Tony couldn't get answers, he at least wanted Johnny's acceptance. This mystery needed some sort of closure.

Johnny stared at the glasses deep in wonder. He did not make eye contact with his friend and instead, took the opportunity to distance himself.

The sounds of a grim wind continued to shout at the sky above, blowing and sounding longer than it had before.

For Johnny, bits of information were suddenly coming together to make more sense than they had previously, for it wasn't all that long ago the two friends battled a demon in a German cathedral. Stranger things had happened in the young men's lives and the unbelievable was suddenly becoming, at the very least, probable.

After a sound of a mighty crack came the flash of lightning. Through the back window, the light, if only for a short time, sprayed the church office wall, grabbing the immediate attention of the young men.

It caught them both by surprise and they reacted by immediately looking out to the dark grey sky. The fierce wind had the outside trees swaying with vigour.

There was more silence as both friends waited for it and moments later, the sky once again replied to the winds angry howl. The thunderous shout was thick and nearby, closely followed by a few quick streaks and flashes.

This was indeed a severe thunder storm.

Johnny looked back at Tony, but Tony was still in awe at Mother Nature's nasty side. Tony continued to look at the grey sky outside, waiting in anticipation for the next set of flashes.

It kept him intrigued for a little while longer and while it did, it was time for Johnny to say what he had been keeping to himself for some time.

"You know, I have had my fair share of visions and strange occurrences, too. Yes, I believe you."

This grabbed Tony's immediate attention. He broke his stare to look at his friend. He was in awe with what he just heard.

As Tony looked to re-establish an urgent eye to eye connection, Johnny looked away and reached for the sunglasses.

Johnny picked up the glasses and examined them back and front, much in the same way as he had a month earlier when he was first told of Tony's strange, demonic and fiery visions.

He did back then what he was about to do now.

He raised them to his head, holding them at a small distance to his eyes. He slowly bought them forward, eventually wearing them. At all times he kept his fingers on the frames of the glasses. If there were to be any visions then these were going to be removed quicker than the flashes of lightning outside.

Tony eagerly awaited a reaction from his friend.

Something, anything, perhaps a jolt of the head would signify the glasses were playing demonic images for Johnny, maybe a look of shock on his face would suggest there was indeed something sinister about these dark lenses.

The clock ticked by.

Ten seconds, twenty, thirty and nothing.

Not a single response.

Tony waited with anticipation. He was keen.

He so wanted Johnny to experience what could only be described as the horror he had seen on the waterfront a month earlier. Proof would remove any doubt between the two friends, but on this occasion, it wasn't meant to be.

Nothing back then when it first occurred and nothing now.

Johnny wiggled the frames cautiously off his head. They were removed gently and slowly. He then proceeded to hand them over to his friend, but the look on Tony's face was enough to decline the friendly offer.

Those sorts of demonic visions should be limited to once in a lifetime.

Tony had no desire to put these back on his head, ever.

The items were placed back on the desk corner. Johnny left them out of their case for now, sitting upright with the dark lenses staring back towards him. He took a moment longer to make sure they were placed just right so they wouldn't get in the way or fall or get damaged.

They both looked upon them for a little while longer, hoping the lenses would play something or change colour or do anything. Unfortunately, it wasn't meant to be.

Johnny kept them where he could observe them, just like he had with the month just passed. Nothing out of the ordinary had been noted to date.

Tony sat patiently while Johnny rummaged through one of his desk drawers. He brought out a dusty, leathery bound thing.

The book hit the table hard, already open and with Johnny searching through the pages, the text setting was typical of a bible. Written like a tabloid newspaper, there were two columns of text per page, with a book almost as thick as the desk drawer itself.

Johnny continued to flick the pages, he was about two thirds through and he must have been close. He was skim reading, looking to locate a particular set of paragraphs.

And there it was. Johnny tapped his finger on the line of the sentence as if it were a key on a typewriter.

Johnny left his finger there and looked up. There was an intro coming, it only required a bit more thought.

"You and I..." Johnny paused for a moment as he took a big breath as if he were about to make the announcement of his life.

"You and I, we have seen things unnatural. We have fought side by side against demon and sworn to secrecy by the high priests of Europe. If there was ever any doubt in my mind about heaven or hell, I can tell you this is why I sit before you as a servant of God. I am a converted believer. One thousand percent. Heaven and hell exist because we have both taken it on face to face and fist to fist. We have lived through it."

"And it appears we still are living through it," replied Tony. A sad, sarcastic tone resonated in his voice.

"You needn't worry, my friend. You don't need to convince me of your visions, but for me, it's not a matter of whether you saw what you saw, but more so a question of Why? Or better still, why you and me? Let me read you something from this passage."

Johnny's finger hadn't moved and his eyes had quickly re-focussed in on the start of the paragraph of interest.

Tony watched his friend's eyes begin to dance across the sentences and paragraph of the text.

"Be alert, be on the watch! For your enemy, the devil, roams around like a roaring lion, looking for someone to devour. Be aware, for it is you and I that will bear his mark and when we do, the circle of hell will be complete. Satan has fallen to Earth, caught up in his own beauty, power and pride and men will follow blindly, losing the good of intellect only to be replaced with substance of evil."

Johnny skimmed past the next few paragraphs, his finger followed down one page and to the top of the other. He had found what he was looking for as he glanced his eyes upwardly to intro his next reading.

"Take a look at this. There are signs. Definite signs! He is here amongst us."

"He?" asked Tony.

"The devil. Satan! Lucifer! Try and keep up, will you," Johnny replied impatiently and then continued with his intro before his next reading of the text.

"We know it as the apocalypse. I am certain of it. It is here and the dark one walks amongst us. The mark of the beast exists here and now. Many know of or have read about the apocalypse. The Four Horsemen. Plague, pestilence, famine and war. We all know it. Some may even know these are biblical signs that Satan walks amongst us."

Johnny looked at the sky, which at that instant cracked and flashed. The thunderous roar lasted for several seconds, the sound living through the flashes of lightning that followed. The sounds and the brightness appeared to finish at the same time.

"Just a severe winter's thunderstorm that isn't scary, once you understand the mechanics behind how it all works. Science has taken the mystery out of lightning and weather patterns and all these things we take for granted. So as a child, the lightning and thunder is scary; as an adult we are simply cautious about its existence. So when it flashes all around us, some might cower in fear, but many of us just get on with life."

Johnny tapped the pages of his book.

"Same here. Famine, war and all these things. We know they exist. Whether we like it or not, whether we chose to see it or turn a blind eye to it, it's a part of living on this Earth, so I get it. Some read the scriptures of the bible, the apocalypse and the four horsemen and think it's a sign, others are just complacent about its existence. They think nothing more of it. It has become an everyday part of watching the news, an everyday part of living life on Earth. We have all become numb to its existence without a second thought on the matter. So it exists, but there are probably many who would not consider the biblical reference to war and pestilence and so forth. Like the lightning, it happens and we all simply get on with life."

Johnny went back to the text of his book.

"And then there are other signs. This bit! This has me intrigued." He continued with the reading of the text at the bottom of the right hand page.

"Everyone, be them small or great, rich or poor, free or slave will be forced to wear the mark of the beast. To receive a mark on the right hand or on the forehead so that no one can buy or sell, unless he has his mark. A mark which will bear his name or number. A sign Satan is amongst you all."

Johnny then looked up.

"And the number he shall bear is six, six, six."

A small pause followed.

"Pretty standard stuff. Heard it all before. The coming of the four horsemen, the tell-tale signs of the second coming, the mark of the beast." Johnny sarcastically dismissed the evidence he had presented as if it were a light hearted joke.

Johnny got up and left the office to go to the fridge, he opened the door and pulled out a can of cola only to return soon after.

"Take a look at this."

Johnny displayed the barcode at the bottom of the can.

"Yeh, so it's a barcode. So what?" remarked Tony.

"Don't you see it? Take a closer look. The barcode, no matter what the number is, is bordered by two double lines; there is also a similar line in the middle."

Johnny pointed out the three sets of double lines by taking one of the coloured pens out of its holder and using it to emphasize the barcode borders to the left, middle and right of the printed barcode.

"Now these lines all have various thicknesses and patterns, each styling unique to its number. Now see the six here in print, it is represented by two thin lines." Johnny used his pen to highlight the pattern symbolised by this specific number.

"Now look at the borders and the middle line. Look at the pattern they resemble. If a number was going to be attached to these lines then it would be six, six, six."

As Johnny repeated the word six, he pointed to the double line on the left, then the one in the middle and finishing with the double line on the right hand side.

Johnny tapped the borderline to the right a few times, re-emphasising his point, and then looked up.

"I fear the day is near where they barcode the citizens of the world. Tattoo us like the Jews in the Nazi war camps. This will be a day to remember. This will be the day we all come to bear the mark of the beast."

Tony, whilst listening to Johnny, studied the lines on the can of cola.

Johnny continued, "Some may say this is superstitious or coincidental, others may say you make of it what you will, but I truly believe that it will come to be as it is written in the Holy Scriptures."

At that point, Johnny spun his chair around to face the rear church window. Tony's view of his friend was now the back of an office chair and the back of his friend's head.

Johnny stood, still facing away from his friend. He spoke his words with heart felt conviction.

"Whether you choose to believe or not, the signs are there. I know this in my heart. I feel it in every fibre of my being. He is amongst us and for some reason, we are getting our fair share of his reign of terror."

Chapter Seventeen
Charlie's Recovery

In a heavenly plane, up high where only senior angels roam, Zophiel walked side by side with the Holy Mother.

They shared a common feature.

Both spirits emitted a godly light that was warm and comforting, with one significant difference. Zophiel's light was more blinding, with the Virgin Mother emitting a light more likened to a collection of soft candlelight.

A casual stroll through the billowy floor below. Their feet cut through the clouds of white as Zophiel updated the Virgin Mother of the departure of Lucifer and how Satan left his stronghold of heaven to rule down on Earth below.

The Virgin Mother stopped suddenly and looked directly into the brightness emanating from the great seraphim angel. Unlike many ex-human spirits, a soul of her hierarchy and status wasn't blinded by Zophiel; she was after all, the Queen of angels.

"If he wasn't born to the world then where is he?" asked the Virgin Mother.

"Time is of the essence, Mother. He has left his army to reign over heaven and wishes to begin his reign on Earth. Mother, this has not gone to our expectations. If he was born as infant then the delays in growing and developing from baby to child to man would take far too long. Instead, rather than starting his life out as a newborn, I know this."

Zophiel paused for a brief moment. "He has chosen to possess the body of a young child."

"Possess?" she asked curiously.

"Yes, Mother, don't you see? Essentially he has bypassed the infant years and is in a position to begin planning on his evil reign immediately. Possessed by the unholy disciple of Satan, as a young child, Lucifer will develop the networks he needs to bring havoc into the world below. Along his journey of growth, any good that gets in his way will be eliminated. Anything he finds that will serve his evil purpose will be embraced and nurtured. This is his way."

"I understand, my dear angel, but you have still not answered my question."

"And what is that, my queen."

"So where is he?"

He hated to admit it, but there was no way he could put off the truth any longer. For this bit, the great seraphim looked away from his queen.

"This, we do not know."

~ * ~

Quick action on behalf of Archangel Gabriel made all the difference. Pam and Mary also worked tirelessly to ensure Charlie made a quick and full recovery.

Still weak by his recent encounter with two demonic soldiers, Charlie would be his normal self in next to no time.

Charlie had been pampered and cared for by what appeared to be every angel in heaven. Whilst appreciative of the extra special care, it was important he take some time with his wife.

She needed to understand his experiences, but the place wasn't right. This was a discussion best kept private and so they kept on walking.

Hand in hand making their way through the crowds of spirits and angels, he kept to himself and she lovingly led the way. Charlie's walk was still a little slow, as if he'd had minor abdominal surgery and was walking the hospital wards.

Heaven's healing light would eventually make everything right.

They continued.

She was patient and understanding. He was in no rush.

They avoided any small crowds and purposely walked the other way if approached. The message was clear to leave the loving couple to themselves.

She knew him well enough to let it be for now, but she had to look at him as they casually made their way to a private corner of heaven.

For the moment, Mary grinned at him. It appeared forced and uncomfortable, but at the very least, he returned a loving smile.

Soon after, they were where they wanted to be. Two souls with no one near to disturb them. He turned and faced his wife. She knew better. He'd do all the talking for now.

"I can't tell you how it felt, Mary. The little girl and her mother. We knew that household was trouble from the start. But then, I walk into their room of satanic worship and there they stood; me as surprised as them. They were quick, Mary. There was nothing I could do."

"Don't blame yourself, sweetheart," Mary said, holding the hands of her husband, comfortingly rubbing her thumb on the upper part of his hands and fingers.

"You don't understand, Mary. If it's a fight they want, then bring it on, but not like this."

"Like what?" asked Mary.

"I saw him, Mary. Our Tony, I saw his face as clear as day. In the middle of demonic torture, all I could see was the face of our son."

"Honey, it's not unusual to have your conscious and even your subconscious mind drift to more pleasant thoughts. The only way to not think of the pain and horror of torture is to concentrate on something else. A thought or memory that is comforting, peaceful. It must have been awful for you, but I understand."

"No you don't!"

If there was a gentle way of jerking his hands out of the grip of a loved one, then Charlie had found the solution.

Charlie walked with an injured awkwardness to put a bit more distance between him and his wife and then turned to her.

She was most attentive.

"As they tortured me, for their own sick and demonic amusement, they allowed my son to watch."

Chapter Eighteen
His Demonic Spirit Visits the Church

A few weeks passed and Tony looked forward to catching up with his long-time friend. In recent times their respective lives had kept them busy enough and they had not been able to cross paths, particularly not since they last met to discuss the sunglasses.

In the rear of the church office, Johnny bought in two cups of hot tea and sat in his swivel recliner chair.

Tony nodded his head to where the sunglasses weren't.

"I got sick of seeing them. They're safely tucked away." Johnny tapped his top drawer.

They were safe and sound and put away for another time. Today's discussion would not involve demons, spirits and demonic glasses. Today was one of catch ups.

Sebastian, in spirit, stood to the rear of the church office. A demonic observer in a place of worship. These two friends were as much an enemy to him as they were to Lucifer and his army of evil-doers.

Either way, hell in some way, shape or form, was keeping a close eye on these two.

Sebastian looked to the face of Johnny who was telling his friend about a string of weekend services. A filled Saturday and Sunday of funerals, christenings and weddings.

"Come Sunday night, I was asleep by eight thirty and slept for twelve hours straight. I was knackered!"

Tony laughed and Johnny soon joined in.

With bitterness in his stare, Sebastian stood in his spiritual plane, unamused.

He spoke his evil language out aloud, not that anyone could hear him, but he'd get what he had to get off his conscience.

In screeches and clicks and screams, he cursed at the boys.

"Yes, I'm talking to you. The two of you over there not meeting my eyes for fear I'll see the self-doubt and despair that have begun to edge out your sense of purpose and confidence."

Sebastian's spiritual form could not do much to interrupt the good times the two friends were having.

The two young men were in the middle of a heartfelt laugh, to the point of tears of joy in their eyes. Something Tony had said.

This only stirred up more anger within Sebastian as he looked upon the boys and their merry friendship.

Sebastian snarled at the boys from his demonic plane. The boys were none the wiser.

He then continued to speak in his hellish language.

"Yes, I'm talking to you. The one over there. Carry on with your jokes and pleasantries, but I promise you this, you will not find my vengeance at all amusing."

Sebastian continued on his solo speech as if to make an oath to himself and a commitment to his satanic lord, a promise to himself for he would have his day. Revenge, one way or another, the two young men will pay for everything they had done.

Sebastian looked at Johnny, who was dressed in his church attire. He stared at the neatly pressed white collar, which only angered the demonic warrior even further.

"And you, there in the corner, looking everywhere but at me, afraid to believe your time is almost here." Briefly, Sebastian hissed at the boys.

"Well, it is. You've been working hard, for long years, carving out time, pouring your heart and soul into your work, perfecting your craft and, maybe most important of all, not giving up… But you have no idea."

Sebastian then made eye contact with Johnny who was oblivious to the fact that there was a demon spirit only a few metres from where he sat.

In a snarly tone, Sebastian continued. "So yes, your turn is coming. It's just around the corner there where you can't see it, but it's heading your way. It might be here in two weeks, two months or maybe two years, but it will be here."

Sebastian paused only long enough to have a long and heartfelt laugh to himself. A laugh that was eerily sinister in nature.

He then, before returning to his troops in his captured heaven, shouted his final words. The boys did not hear, but Sebastian had his final say; this was directed to Johnny, the last bit spoken in the language of English.

"You!" a pause for only a second or two as he began his phasing in and out for his journey onward to the heavenly plane.

The spiritual echo remained within the church walls long after Sebastian departed. It still only remained audible for spiritual audiences, but none-the-less, had been left to reverberate for a little longer.

Its sound loud and its message demonically clear, it stated, "YOUR SOUL IS MINE!"

Chapter Nineteen
My Little Allie

Shortly before his death, Jesus Christ gave this warning to his disciples: "What I say to you I say to all. Keep on the watch!"

~ * ~

As the sun rose and dawn broke, the sky began its bath in yellowy hues. For an instant as the colour of the sky shifted, a salmon pink haze danced across the landscape.

Allie sat on the outside chair. She had been sitting there for close to three hours.

Little girls should not be by themselves and out in the early hours of the morning, let alone the dark hours of the night.

Allie's head wobbled side to side, casually as if she were on some hallucinogenic drug. She remained in her meditative state for a little bit longer, unaware of all around.

As the sun's rays warmed the cold of her cheeks, she opened her eyes, alert and ready for the day ahead.

Stretching and yawning, she sat in her front porch chair, admiring the early signs of sunrise and all the subtle colour changes of the skies.

Two mid-sized dogs in the near distance caught her eyes. They approached one another from opposite sides of the street; one a mixture of brown and white, the other an all-black dog. Both were of similar height with the black dog being of a sturdier build.

Their breeds were a mix, mongrels of a sort, and Allie had seen them both previously, wandering around the suburban streets from time to time.

The dogs approached each other with teeth snarling.

Allie watched on with a quirky smile.

In next to no time, the dogs were interlocked, snarling and growling. Both were on their hind legs, with front legs high and bodies interlocked, their respective heads shifting in and out, looking for a way to bite and maim.

For a little while, the fight was even, each giving out as much as it got, but then the brown and white dog shifted its body to the right. For a split second, it saw the top part of the black dog's neck and latched on with all of its might.

It sunk its teeth in fast and hard as the black dog let out a mighty yelp and quickly shook itself free.

The black dog ran off, a gaping wound turning its black fur into red and then dripping down its trail for all to see. The little pools of blood continued to hit the bitumen road as the black dog accepted his agonizing defeat.

The brown and white dog, having settled from its fight, turned to look at the only human spectator in the street.

Allie looked at it and the dog looked back.

Allie's quirky smile had been replaced with an intense look of abomination.

The dog steadied his stance and showed his teeth, the snarls were coming out in short bursts followed by short pauses. This pattern continued for a small amount of time.

The dog's snarling lengthened, pausing only to catch another deep breath, ready for its next extended growl.

Allie kept her sights on the dog and the dog returned the look with teeth bared.

Suddenly, Allie's eyeballs turned a fireball red as if someone had poured kerosene within her eye sockets and set them alight. The orangey red was brighter than ever as her demonic glare went through to the core of the canine.

A split second later, the brown and white dog was running down the street, yelping louder and longer than the dog it just fought with.

It left the vicinity as quick as it could, the cries of pain subsiding as it got farther and farther away.

The silence of the early hours of the morning were back again, only to be broken by a mother's search for her little daughter.

Soon the front door swung open and Angela stepped out to see her Allie sitting in the front porch chair.

"So that's where you're hiding, my little devil." Angela spoke excitedly as any mother would speak to their child. Her tones were high and fun-like.

Angela then stepped out to hold the door open. She bowed her head slightly as one might when addressing royalty.

Still speaking with her young daughter, Angela's mannerism changed to a more serious, definitive discussion, speaking as if she were formerly addressing an Admiral in the navy.

She allowed the body of her daughter to walk past her as she spoke her words.

"Please come inside, my Dark Lord, your breakfast is getting cold."

Chapter Twenty
Johnny the Prophet

Archangels Michael, Gabriel and the angel Raphael stayed to the back of the church, hovering mid-air in their spiritual world. Pam was also there as she floated above the ground, surrounded by her three angelic friends.

On this Saturday afternoon, Johnny finished his last service for the day, a baptism for a baby boy. A private sermon with a small group of close families and friends. Twenty four heads in all attended.

They were now gone and the church was in need of a quick tidying before tomorrow's regular Sunday service.

The rest had been swept and cleaned, the altar left to prepare.

Johnny laid the cloth down and neatly placed his icons, crucifixes and Christian ornaments on his bench top to display and show them off to the crowds of tomorrow.

"This one is special to us," remarked the archangel Michael.

Pam couldn't be prouder of a former neighbour she had known since his birth. She watched him grow into a young man on Earth and cared for his wounds in heaven at a time when he and Tony completed their angelic mission into hell.

Pam had also promised herself that on that one day when Johnny and Tony would meet that time in their lives where all bodily functions cease and the soul makes that magical transition to a higher plane, then at that time, she would make sure they knew what they had done with their times in heaven.

She was entrusted to ensure Tony and Johnny remembered, but she also hoped they would both enjoy long and fulfilling lives before then.

The angels stood there in silence and Pam remained in the middle of the three angelic beings.

She was puzzled.

"So why are we here?" she asked.

"People on Earth have grown frustrated and have turned from using the gift of God within them," stated Raphael.

"On Earth as it is in heaven. When heaven suffers, then the chaos will spill over onto those who walk the Earth. This is the result of a heaven run by demons," said the archangel Michael.

With a firm and direct tone, Raphael spoke. "We cannot wait any longer! It is time we take action to get those pure of heart and spirit into the spotlight. Guide them in a way only we know how, so they can take charge and lead by example."

"We wish to reconnect the people to God." Gabriel spoke calmly as he put his comforting arm around the angel Raphael.

Indeed, it had been troubling times for all, especially the angelic hierarchy having lost the only home they ever knew to a satanic leader and his army of demons.

"And we shall make him a prophet. We will guide his path and he shall speak the words of God, more so than he does as a preacher man. He will teach and lead his people in ways unimaginable to him now. He will do so as we direct him to," added the archangel Gabriel.

"You will be given the task of being his spirit guide. It is through visitation, prophecy, vision and dreams that Johnny will lead the way for his congregation. The people of this world need to be born again, to re-believe and be re-acquainted with their holy spirit. The people of this world need to distinguish between what is clean and what is unclean, distinguish between the heavenly realm and the demonic," said the archangel Michael.

"We must equip this preacher man to know how to respond to the outpouring of the Lord's spirit, how to receive heavenly visitations and minister in the prophetic. One as pure in spirit and soul can only then pass on these messages to lead his people back into one of reconnecting with their heaven," added Gabriel.

As passionate as one could be, Raphael spoke. "To neglect this duty is to invite disaster."

Pam responded. "I have my fullest confidence that Johnny will teach all how to work with the angels. I know this young man back to front and inside out." She then paused for a second as she repositioned her stature to stand tall and strong.

"He will do us all proud," she said with an immense feeling of pride bursting out of her soul.

In unison, the three angels raised their angelic arms and gently rested them on Pam's shoulders.

The three angels then spoke their words simultaneously.

"He already has!"

Chapter Twenty-one
A Christmas in Adelaide

In this year of nineteen ninety two, Christmas was only a few working days away. This year, the holy celebration fell on a Friday and the summer was like any other, with the country turning their clocks back to enjoy daylight savings, to enjoy evening falling a little later than it had in the winter and autumn months.

And normally, the extra evening hours would encourage the masses to spend their time outdoors, but where there is sun there is also heat.

In the city of Adelaide, a recent heatwave had put many off from walking the malls and streets of the city's shopping districts; the temperature more fitting to being by cool beach water or staying indoors in a home fitted with a well powered air conditioner.

Seven days straight with temperatures soaring above the old century mark had made it uncomfortable for all, but a recent change in direction for the wind meant it no longer blew hot air off the inland Australian desert, but rather, blew northerly, taking with it cooler air off the southern seas.

A cooler warmth engulfed the city of Adelaide this afternoon and with it came a massive splurge of people hitting the streets for their last minute shopping. Temperatures today were considerably more comfortable than in recent times.

The paved mall, the main shopping district of Adelaide, ran a length to satisfy even the fussiest of shoppers. At a little over half a kilometre long, a selection of multi and single storey shops of all shapes and sizes bordering its wide pathway, many of the retailers fittingly displaying their festive lights and decorations.

Some Christmas ornaments were small and quaint, others large and colourful.

Amongst the bigger of the decorations was a two storey tall Santa which hung off the outside wall belonging to one of the larger retail shops located in the middle of the mall. A hundred metres east, another popular retailer had seven gigantic leaves of mistletoe positioned as if they were gently floating to the ground. The leaves had been placed up on the outside wall of the seventh level, spaced evenly all the way down to the second floor. Positioned on one of Adelaide's oldest department stores, it was a decoration that had been put on for the festive season year after year.

The general public of Adelaide had quickly become accustomed to these large decorations. The placing of them was a must for young and old to enjoy. Made in a colourful plastic, there was no mistaking Santa was in town and only a few department doors down, he had bought along with him his mistletoe, floating from the seventh to the second storey. There they were for all to see, with their ever-green leaves bordered with their distinct red berries.

It was exceptionally busy with hordes of people of all ages walking up and down and in and out of shops, the mall also filled with many buskers.

There was hardly enough room for the street acts, but they managed to find their space, their songs and performing antics breaking up the muffled sound of thousands of conversations.

As the sun set into the early evening, the tall building's deepening shadows grew across the paved mall until the dark of night was almost near, a gentle warmth still lingering in the air.

As the sun lowered, the moon rose. Tonight would be something special, as the night time put on a heavenly light show.

The enlarged moon cast an ethereal glow over the city of Adelaide. The moon was orbiting close to the Earth tonight, as many stargazers would observe it's full and larger than usual appearance.

It was a surreal setting to a special city district night.

Suddenly at eight pm precisely, at the eastern end of the mall, the lamps and shop lights dimmed. The bells of a city's nearby church chimed as hundreds upon hundreds of shoppers stopped to enjoy the up and coming early evening spectacle.

Today, the church bell would not strike eight times for the hour but would ring for the symbolic twelve days of Christmas.

After its twelfth chime, the church bells stopped and for a minute, all that could be heard was the sound of those at the western end of the mall rushing to get closer to the approaching musical show.

Tony was in a prime position to take in this Christmas spectacle. Standing alone in the crowd, he waited for this city's popular festive celebration to begin.

Like Tony, many of the city's people had paused from their partying with friends or shopping for presents.

All eyes turned skywards, but many were no longer looking at the enlarged moon. Instead, all eyes were fixed on the city's choir and twenty piece orchestra, situated on the upper balcony, the selection of musicians and singers could be seen from below by shoppers close and afar.

They would soon play a selection of popular Christmas carols.

The silent pause continued for a little while longer as the crowd below finally settled into their positions, the musicians and singers at the ready.

Then the spotlights suddenly appeared; their reds, greens and white slicing through the deep purple of night.

The spotlights danced across the mall below, weaving in and out, each colour crossing over with the other. The lights danced and intermingled, entertaining the audiences below.

Before too long, the organ music began to play its intro, a melody of notes lingered only for a short time and then the horn, flute, lute and harp joined in. Within a musical bar or two, a children's choir hummed, their young soprano voices making for a background to the coming hymns.

The adult choir was ready. Soon their voices would override their younger counterparts, breaking straight into the classical carol of 'Silent Night'.

The colourful lights shone below and continued with their dance.

They finished their first song, the cheer from below quickly followed. The next carol started soon after.

'Joy to the World'. The opening verse was simply angelic. The musicians played their instruments, their pitch and tone so perfect as to not drown out the beauty in the voices of the adult and child choir.

They had barely got past their second chorus and Tony had seen and heard enough, his mind more preoccupied with the task at hand. The shops would close soon and there was a critical piece of shopping left. He could no longer afford the time to stop for the niceties of a city's Christmas concert.

It was slow going as Tony navigated outward through the dense crowd. The shop he sought was nearby.

He finally got there, entering a major department store with a bag in either hand. He'd already bought his gifts for his family, the final purchase and difficult choice was for his long-time friend, Johnny.

Johnny was not one to receive gifts, a modern day priest who did not mingle in the materialistic world, but how could Tony not buy his best friend a Christmas present.

It had to be something special, perhaps sentimental in some way.

He couldn't settle on what to buy and continued on his search in hope that gazing across endless shelves filled with infinite items would give him some type of inspiration.

He was not alone.

In the spiritual plane, they had just appeared.

He was closely followed by his deceased parents.

Despite the hectic numbers of shoppers, the parents' heavenly eyes were fixed on their only son.

Tony got off the escalator on level one and turned right. Soon after he was stopped by a sales assistance who'd setup a display bench near enough to the escalators exit.

"Sir, take a smell of the new range of aftershave," she said, intruding on Tony's privacy.

"This one we call, Feuille De Chene. It's the French word for oak leaf. You may sense it has a subtle, woody, oaky fragrance, with a hint of spring flowers." Her voice very dynamic and captivating.

The shop assistant sprayed a small piece of absorbent paper with the men's cologne and waved the paper in the air to settle the smell. She then handed it to Tony.

"What do you think?" she said playfully.

Tony liked the smell, but Johnny wasn't exactly into men's fragrances and Tony was not going to spend any more than he had set out to.

"It's nice, but I am going to have to say no."

The female assistant persisted. "You are welcome to try some on yourself, the fragrance and flowery smells settle better on human skin." The assistant knew every angle from which to promote her wares.

She reached out, gesturing Tony give her his arm, but Tony refused.

"I'm sorry, but I am in a bit of a hurry." Tony was polite but direct.

"Thank you, sir, then enjoy your shopping and a Merry Christmas to you."

"Thank you, and to you and yours, a Merry Christmas."

Tony was on his way again, but not before the keen female shop assistant had snagged her next unsuspecting male shopper; her opening pitch exactly the same as the one she had used on him.

Tony nodded his head ever so slightly as he left the area as if to say, 'Poor fella, she got you as well.'

Soon Tony was back at glancing at the shelves and walking from one end of the store to the other.

His deceased parents were never too far away, although Tony was none the wiser.

"Isn't it wonderful news about Mum?" Mary couldn't be prouder.

"It's about time! The people in this world need to reconnect with their spiritual side," Mary added. "And who better to help than Mum. Mum will help Johnny to help the people of his community."

Charlie and Mary didn't have to navigate the crowds; they walked straight through them. Unfortunately, the same could not be said for Tony who weaved and dodged shopper after shopper, making his way around and from one end of a shopping floor to other and from one level to the next to the next.

The spiritual parents were never too far behind as they continued to keep a watchful eye on their son.

Tony turned a corner and had stopped on the third floor, in a book section of the department store. Tony casually picked up a book, flicked through its pages, and put it down, doing the same for a number of books and magazines. Topics wide and varied had passed through the hands of Tony. Fictional and non-fiction, it kept him busy as he gazed across the endless selection of reading materials.

Every now and then, Tony stopped to read something in a little more depth before moving onto and inspecting his next. An article or paragraph here and there grabbing his attention, but only for a little while. Before too long, the publication was placed back on its shelf and Tony was quickly onto flicking through his next hard cover or magazine.

Mary and Charlie stood side by side and a few metres back looking to the rear of their son. Tony moved into the sports reading section and was onto a fishing magazine, lost in one of the many articles on fishing adventures and paraphernalia.

In the short time they had been following their son, Mary and Charlie had stood or walked side by side and kept a little bit of distance between them and their son.

And up until now, Mary had done all of the talking.

As the parents both stood in the book section of the store, Mary took her eyes off her son to look at her husband, his eyes still fixed on Tony and his gaze somewhat aloof.

She knew him well enough to know there was something he wanted to say. She paused, waiting for him to speak, all along keeping a caring stare on her husband.

It must have been obvious Mary was staring, although Charlie did not turn his head to look at her.

This concern of his had been brewing within him for some time. With a nervousness in his voice, he felt the time was right to off-load.

"It still bugs me, Mary." The worry written all over Charlie's face. "I cannot get it out of my head. Why would they allow Tony to watch whilst those sons of Lucifer play with my soul, torture me for their own satanic pleasures?"

Mary kept to her silence.

"I worry for Tony. I feel it in me. Those demons are out for our son," said Charlie. "There is something sinister in the making," he added.

"Like what?" asked Mary.

"I don't know. I can't say for certain. It's a feeling I have deep inside me. Gnawing at me like a dog to a bone. It's been like that ever since I got attacked."

Charlie and Mary stopped their talking for now. They watched Tony put down his fishing magazine only to find a publication on the martial arts.

This was a special edition which covered the world of self-defence from all parts of the world.

A special little "in the years gone by" type story about a world tournament held in Munich, Germany. This was a competition Johnny and Tony had both travelled overseas to attend.

The author of this article had captured the competition highlights well. He wrote of the classic fights, the upsets, and the injuries and gave an overview on a competition that ran like clockwork. The Germans would set the standard for future fighting competitions.

As Tony read the article it was like he and Johnny were sitting in their seats again, absorbing every bit of competition atmosphere, watching the fighters go for gold.

Tony was into the third page of this eight page article, a story filled with endless text and many colourful photos. Before reading his next paragraph, his mind was made up. This was going to be his gift to Johnny; in part, a happy and reminiscent memory of their trip and holiday abroad.

Tony read on. He would make the purchase once he had read the article of the championships tournament in the town of Munich, Germany.

In the spiritual world, Charlie turned to make eye contact with his wife.

"I don't know if there is a sinister demon on the prowl. I couldn't say if it's the demon Sebastian or Lucifer himself. It may even be another one of Lucifer's followers. I have this threatening feeling within me that speaks strongly of actions of harm and danger to our son."

"Why didn't you speak to me before about this?" asked Mary.

"I didn't know what to think. I had just come off a demonic beating, I wasn't in a right state of mind," pleaded Charlie. But things are clearer now. The memory and anguish of being tortured by those demons doesn't bother me as much as it had done in recent times. With heaven's help, as time has passed, I lost the connection of emotion to those memories. I'm nearly healed, Mary, and I feel as good as I ever have, but my previous feelings of anguish have been replaced with this gut-feeling concern. It burns within me, I can't explain it and I am not entirely sure I understand it, but if I had to put some sort of meaning to it, then it would speak of harm to our son."

Mary's maternal instinct stepped in. She now worried for both her husband's intuition and her son's safety. She walked over to Tony who was still deeply involved in his fighting competition article. She longed to hug and hold her son, but the best she could manage was to wrap her spiritual arms around his body and imagine a mother and son embrace. Although she could not physically touch him, Mary sought to connect with the soul of her son and in a way, she must have.

Tony instantly stopped his reading.

In amongst the shoppers of the floor, Tony stood tall, his eyes fixed to a distant wall. A spiritual shiver ran through his being, like a cold chill on a winter's night. It brought goose bumps to his forearms as his hairs stood on their ends. *'How strange,' he must be thinking*, thought Mary. The shop air conditioning made the ambient temperature of the third floor comfortable, not too cold and not too hot, but for a second or two, Tony was shivering as if he were standing naked in the snow.

The sensation settled as quickly as it started and Tony thought nothing of it and went back to his reading, Mary still in her spiritual embrace.

Charlie stood back, watching his wife give their son a spiritual hug. Charlie maintained a watchful eye on his family. He would protect them no matter what the cost.

Charlie spoke the words he had been keeping to himself since the demonic attack. He made sure Mary understood his nagging feelings of concern.

Mary wished she could be there to protect Tony. Instead, she maintained her imaginary embrace as she turned her head to face her husband.

With spiritual husband and wife now locked in concerning eye contact, Charlie spoke. "Something evil is in the making and I fear our Tony is going to be in its line of fire."

Chapter Twenty-two
The Second Coming

All up, the church helpers were made up of eighteen adults. They were from the surrounding suburbs, a local community which supported their church as often as they could manage.

Every Sunday, they gave their priest a helping hand. Everything from singing the hymns, gathering money donations and any other miscellaneous church-bound duties was all part of donating their time and service as Sunday help.

This group, mature in age, ranged from a dedicated male Christian in his late thirties through to an elderly lady in her seventieth year. The older lady had her health issues and attended infrequently. The male, on the other hand, never missed a sermon. The others tried to make it as often as they could, but either way there was always a group of helpers around the place to assist with the duties of a Sunday service.

Today, all the helpers were present.

Their voices sang out the last few choruses of the hymn as Johnny sat in a chair located to the wall behind the altar. The chair, dedicated to the priest of the church, was frequently used by Johnny when the choir sung its songs or when others in the church community were called upon to present a talk or to read from the Holy Scriptures.

Johnny would normally use this time to relax his mind and sort out his thoughts, but today was different.

In his mind, Johnny shut out the choir and background noises and replaced them with self-talk to mentally psyche himself up for a sermon that warranted exaggeration in the voice, warranted demand and dynamic speech.

Today, he would put on the show of his life.

His heart pumped a little harder as the adrenaline hit his bloodstream. His throat went a little dry, but nothing a few hard swallows wouldn't fix.

Soon, he would have his moment in the spotlight.

Johnny stood, dressed in his clergy attire, and walked towards the altar waiting for the last note of the hymn to draw to a conclusion.

The choir finished and Johnny turned his head in acknowledgement of a job well done.

He then faced his congregation, a full house of people of all ages. He took a moment or two as he flicked the pages of his bible to the marked spot, his talk today drawing on the writings of the 'Second Coming.'

His training as a priest and years of dedicating himself to the sport of martial arts and meditation all came together to serve a purpose of a focussed mindset. He took a deep breath and was about to deliver a speech in a way which was outside his comfort zone, but he was determined to deliver it in a way which he had been planning all week. Be it to say, he had never done anything in this manner before but he was about to give it his all. All psyched for the occasion, he projected his booming voice forward. The opening paragraph designed to capture the attention of his audience and capture it, he did.

"For the Lord himself will come down from heaven, with a loud command, with the voice of the archangel and with the trumpet call of God. And the dead in Christ will rise first, after that, we who are still alive and are left will be caught up together with them in the clouds to meet the Lord in the air. And so we will be with the Lord forever. This, my good people, is the Second Coming of our Lord, Jesus Christ."

Johnny was pleased, at the very least, he got their attention.

"So what of the dead, you ask!"

Johnny held his breath and stood stationary as if he had been frozen still in time. The moment only lasted a few seconds, but the outcome was what he wanted—emphasis and dramatics.

He drew on this silence for a little while longer, his congregation now all ears, not knowing what to expect next"

"How can the dead be raised to life?" he said, projecting his voice louder than he had done only moments before.

A normality returned to his voice, speaking as if in conversation with another.

"What kind of body will they have? Have you ever wondered that in order for a plant to sprout to life, the seed must die? You plant, perhaps a grain of wheat, or some other kind, not the full bodied plant that will grow up."

With his finger pointed to the sky, "God provides the seed with the body he wishes, and the flesh of living beings is not the same kind of flesh. Men have one kind of flesh, fish another, birds another as will the flesh of the dead."

He bought his arm down and paused to gauge his audience. He had them in his hands and judging by some of the faces on some of the people, he had a few scared out of their minds as well.

"This is how it will be when the dead are raised to life. When the body is buried it is mortal; when raised it will be immortal. When buried it is ugly and weak; when raised it will be beautiful and strong. When buried it will be of physical form, when raised—spiritual."

Then Johnny stopped and drew in a big breath, made his body as broad and as inflated as he could.

His voice burst out with vibrancy as passionate as any could be.

"This is what I mean, my good people. What is made of flesh and blood cannot share in God's Kingdom and what is mortal cannot possess immortality."

Then Johnny leaned in a little as if he were going to whisper into someone's ear, however his voice was loud enough for the crowd to hear.

"Listen to this secret," he stated. We shall not all die, but in an instant we shall all be changed, as quickly as the blinking of an eye, when the last angelic trumpet sounds. For when it sounds, the dead will be raised immortal beings and we shall change. For what is mortal must clothe itself with what is immortal; what will die must clothe itself with what cannot die. So when what is mortal has been clothed with what is immortal, and when what will die has been clothed with what cannot die, then the scripture will come true: Death is destroyed, victory is complete!

"In other words, all is not lost, my good people, for at the end of this period, when death no longer exists and the living share the Earth with the undead then as it is written in the scriptures, they will see the Son of Man coming in a cloud with power and great glory. Until the time when the trumpets peal out and the announcement is made that He is to reveal himself, finally, in His Second Coming, then all will feel the joy and peace which has been promised to you through Christ the Lord. Then and only then will all suffering as we know it come to an end. And at this time there is only one thing to do."

Johnny raised his arms as if he were holding a giant ball to the back of his neck and above his shoulders. His head tilted back slightly, his irises centred and raised, his vision looking directly to the ceiling line of his church.

"Now when these things begin to happen, look up and everyone lift your heads."

Johnny kept his arms outstretched, but shifted his vision to his crowd. There was fire in his eyes and love in his heart as he made his final point.

"Because your redemption..." Johnny stopped in mid-sentence and reworded his opening remark.

"You need to be saved from a lifetime of sin and error and evil. You need to be converted to a life of a good and God-loving Christian. This is something that must already be in place. It may not be perfected, but it must exist. And if you reach deep down into your soul and ask your heart of hearts, 'Does it exist?' If the answer to this question comes back to you with any degree of uncertainty then don't miss out. Begin the process and put in place what must exist."

He spoke his final words as lovingly as he could present them.

"Because if we wish to spend our eternity in heaven, then time is running out. We must take action now for it will be too late if left to the final minute. Leave here today knowing that the need to redeem and convert yourselves, is NOW!"

Chapter Twenty-three
The Sunday Gathering

Pam stood in the spiritual world watching and listening to Johnny's all inspiring talk on the 'Second Coming of Jesus Christ.'

"We shall not all die, but in an instant we shall all be changed," she heard him say.

Pam recalled on Tuesday gone by, Johnny was up late and she was working in her spiritual way alongside him. She placed images and heavenly phrases in his subconscious mind.

Johnny looked so tired then.

He'd fallen asleep on the kitchen table, with pen pushed to one side and scrap pieces of paper littered across the floor around him.

There were notes everywhere, a few bullet points on one piece of paper, another a short paragraph, one notation was written on a napkin with only one word scrawled across it in large lettering. It was written in capital letters with three exclamation marks. It read "UNDEAD!!!"

All the notes had an importance to them; the challenging part was piecing them together.

Pam remembered with a little smirk on her ghostly face, Tuesday had got the better of Johnny and Pam thought she would help with a little subconscious sorting of her own.

When he woke an hour later, Johnny was a little more refreshed and was able to put together some of what she was hearing now.

And what Johnny would never know is Pam had done her bit, done what the angels had asked of her. She stayed with Johnny in the week gone past and as he worked on his sermon, Pam worked on him in the only way she knew how.

Spiritually and with heavenly guidance.

She communicated with him subliminally, led his mind to put down words that would form the backbone of today's sermon.

Pam worked on everything from the words to the delivery. Her hard work (and his), she was now listening to. It came together perfectly, she had heard him rehearse in front of the mirror several times over, but now the time had come to put practice into play.

Pam stood in the church's main entrance, a foyer no bigger than the length and width of two standard car park spaces. In all this time Pam had not moved from this spot, looking forward through the main archway.

All that was visible to Pam was a house of prayer, full to the brim. Back of heads everywhere. The congregation was attentive and alert to Johnny as he put his closing touches on his speech.

Johnny stood behind his altar with his flock hanging on every letter of every word. Pam watched the many expressions on Johnny's face as he delivered the Christian message. She proudly watched on as Johnny charismatically put his points forward with flair and pizazz, far better than he had done in any of his practice sessions.

Pam knew today's sermon would be delivered in a way that was exaggerated, bright, vibrant and convincing. She worked hard on Johnny to make him realise for today, he would get out of his comfort zone and preach like he had never preached before. He had to have the crowd from the very first word he spoke and that he did.

Pam clasped her hands and placed them tight up against her heart line. She was excited for Johnny and couldn't be prouder of a young man she'd known his whole lifetime.

There Pam stood alone in the foyer watching it unfold and at the same time, reminiscing of a good week's work. Soon she'd witness all her efforts (and his) come to a conclusion.

Pam had inspired and Johnny had delivered.

In spirit, her feet hovered a little above the foyer's wooded floor. No one could see her ghostly appearance but she could see everything. The floor, still spick-and-span but a little dirtied by a crowd of people entering over an hour ago. Its light tan stain and clear coat looking as good as new.

One wall of this foyer tastefully decorated with a solitary painting, large and bordered by a thick golden wooded frame. The picture was as Christian as it gets, with Jesus Christ on a cross, his bearded face tilted to one side, the 'Crown of Thorns' tightly wrapped around his lifeless forehead.

It got Pam's attention if only for a few seconds.

She noticed the specks of blood which added to the dramatics of the picture. Small pools of red painted on where the nails pierced his hands and feet. The 'Crown of Thorns' left his brown, lengthy hair blood stained with trails of darkened red running down to one side of his cheek.

She looked below the solitary picture to see a tiny book shelf for the pamphlets and church notifications.

Pam was quick to return her attention to Johnny's sermon.

Her spiritual form continued to hover a little above the ground, in the middle of this spacious foyer.

Apart from the picture and book stand there was only one other item in this area.

A stoup for the holy water.

The years had got the better of the stoup whose white had dulled to a very light grey. Little cracks and imperfections could be seen throughout the statue.

It stood waist high and was shaped like an angelic child, their small sets of wings were spread and arms were extended upwardly holding the bowl. The oval dome shape only two inches deep and able to hold enough holy water for the regular congregation.

Either way, and with all of its flaws, many simply commented time and time again, that age and imperfection added to its character and charm and besides that, it looked sturdy enough to serve the people of the church for another hundred years.

Johnny's talk came to an end and as the choir sung their closing hymn, Johnny walked to take his place at the front of the church building.

He walked the middle aisle, acknowledging the people to his left and to his right. His head swung casually from one side of the church to the other, trying to acknowledge as many faces as he could.

All along, he walked a steady pace and Pam could see by the look on his face that he was also pleased with his efforts of today.

Pam stood there smiling as Johnny unknowingly approached her spiritual form. He stopped to dabble his fingers in the holy water, turned to face his altar and did his cross.

Johnny then turned and walked straight through Pam's spiritual form.

He got outside and positioned himself near the main doors. He would soon say his farewells to his crowd as they exited. Pam moved for the first time in a long while to re-position herself to stand next to Johnny.

Johnny was in his place, as was Pam, as they heard the harmonic sounds of the final chorus ring out from within.

The Sunday service was officially concluded and immediately on its finishing came the muffled sound of movement. People got up from their seats and shuffled around. Conversation began as some caught up with old acquaintances, others made their way to the exit.

Soon, his flock casually walked by the main church archway, through the foyer and then passed the main doors of the church.

Many stopped, as had Johnny, to dip their fingers in the holy water and perform their cross.

As the many exited, the occasional someone stopped to have a brief chat with their priest, but mostly, Johnny gave his traditional "And may God be with you," and the people replied, "And with you."

A typical Sunday's finish to an atypical Sunday's service.

~ * ~

As the Sunday morning sermon came to its conclusion, in a home not too far away, Angela and Allie sat in their demonic room of worship.

Allie's body possessed the souls of two forms. Her own soul as well as that of the devil. This child happily lived a life with souls standing and working side by side in a sort of demonic harmony.

Together, Lucifer utilised Allie's physical and spiritual form which would eventually and ultimately deliver his way of evil and destruction to mankind.

But this would be in years to come; she was too young to do so now. The important part for now was to develop her into a lady who could enter into the workforce, work quickly towards position of importance and power.

From here, Lucifer could take over his human host to carry out his reign of terror.

And Lucifer was certain of it; in her adult form she would become more formidable than any could imagine, but until then, her mother would be there as protector, aide and guide.

And in this evil plan in the making, Angela was as dedicated to Lucifer as she was to being the mother of her evil child. Angela considered it a privilege to be part of the demonic plan and she would give her life to ensure that no danger came to her daughter and evil master.

Allie and Angela sat on their four large grey cushions, set down on the wooded floor below. With legs crossed, backs upright and hands placed upwardly, resting on their knees, they sat there with eyes loosely fixed on the black wall.

In the late of morning, the curtains were drawn and the door shut. The light in the room was dim. Mother and daughter sat comfortably on their cushions, turning to face the symbols on one of the walls.

They stared at the dark red, the demons number of six, six, six painted in a triangular fashion with the tails of the numbers all pointed to the centre. The sixes stretched out to the entire length and width of the wall.

Both Allie and Angela were in a meditative, trance-like state, their gaze fixed to the centre of the devil's number.

Lucifer's spiritual form emerged from Allie whilst the physical form of Allie slumped over.

Angela snapped out of her trance and immediately bowed to her demonic master and then got up to position her daughter's slumped body into a more comfortable position. She gently laid her young head on one of her cushions and stretched her body out.

She left the demonic room, be it briefly, to retrieve a heavy woollen blanket for her daughter and a thick pullover for herself.

Somewhere between leaving and re-entering the room, the demon Sebastian had made an appearance.

Angela re-entered the room wearing a pink pullover. Angela stopped to acknowledge Sebastian, a subtle bow of her head and Sebastian returned a similar greeting.

Angela could already feel the room get colder and didn't hesitate on placing the grey coloured blanket on her unconscious daughter. Misty vapour formed as both mother and daughter exhaled.

Angela bent over, a final adjustment of the blanket, ensuring Allie was covered from the base of her chin to the tips of her toes. Angela then stood, clasping her hands together to blow some warmth into her fingers. The chill had taken over the room, but measures had been taken to keep warm.

In the spiritual world stood the demonic warrior Sebastian and his master Lucifer, in the physical world were Angela and her unconscious daughter.

For a short moment, before conversation was to begin, the three entities glanced their eyes over the sleeping body of Allie.

The moment didn't last long and soon the evil trio went onto their business.

The conversation began, an evil plan about to unfold.

Lucifer led the discussion.

In a demanding voice he stated, "The one they call Johnny." Lucifer paused briefly to look both Sebastian and Angela squarely in the eye. "This mortal that lives life as a priest, His time has come. Get rid of him!"

Chapter Twenty-four
Chance Meeting

It was early Sunday afternoon and Johnny was still on a high from his sermon a few hours back.

Johnny made himself a sandwich in the small kitchen/office area located in a small room tucked in a corner of the church. A late lunch, something simple. He chewed on his bread, ham and cheese as he revisited an article from the magazine Tony had gifted him not long ago.

He fed his hungry stomach and settled his excited mind from a sermon well executed. And what better way to relax than with a magazine whose contents were about a very familiar karate competition.

He looked over the many pictures of the karate tournament he had the good fortune to be a spectator at. This competition was held in the German town of Munich and Johnny couldn't help but re-read selected paragraphs and gaze over the many photographs.

It was a heartfelt stroll down memory lane for him. Johnny read his articles and enjoyed his sandwich, every chew taken with a smile on his face.

Pam was floating carefree in another area, drifting high above the pews with no-one but the church furniture and walls for company.

Being on Earth around former family and friends was comforting to Pam. It gave her a break from heaven and in particular, put some space between her and the tensions surrounding the demonic invasion.

Being in a house of worship added the bonus which was heart-warming to anyone whose spiritual soul belonged to God.

When it came to Pam however, spending time around Johnny gave her the best of both worlds, but either way, it was just plain old nice to get away and separate oneself from their heavenly bound duties. Ultimately, everyone deserves a holiday now and then.

Suddenly there was an unexpected knock on the rear door of the church where Johnny sat eating his lunch.

It was a surprise visit from Tony.

Johnny's face lit up when Tony looked over to see his Christmas magazine present open on the table next to a plate and half eaten sandwich. The moment could not pass without comment.

"So you like my Christmas present," he said sarcastically.

Johnny smirked and let his friend in. "Can I fix you a sandwich?"

Tony replied, "Not for me. Just had me a nice big lunch with Grandpa."

Pam heard faint voices in conversation, the tone may have been soft and distant, but it was definitely recognizable.

Without a second to spare, she floated her spiritual form over the church pews as fast as she could, eager to look at the face of her grandson.

How she wished to hold him, but if she could not hold him then she would bathe in his presence for a while.

"And how is your granddad? It's been a little while since I have seen him," asked Johnny.

"Age is getting the better of him, but he's as strong as an ox. Doing well for a man in his eighties. I keep an eye on him and drop in regularly."

"Good to hear. He's a good family man with good ol' fashioned values," replied Johnny.

"I don't know what I'd do without him," Tony added.

Little moments like these made it all worthwhile for Pam. Times where she could get small snippets of information on how her family was going. Times where she could check in on loved ones and see they were all okay or at the very least, as well as could be expected.

Pam hung around while Tony and Johnny had their catch up. The surprise visit turned into casual chit chat which lasted a little over an hour.

The hour seemed to pass like minutes for Pam, but as they say, all good things must come to an end. Tony said his goodbyes and Johnny shut the door and went to tidy up in the church's kitchen.

Pam had enjoyed the company and now that Johnny was alone again, she went back to doing what she had done before, but this time floated in and around the foyer and front archway.

Only a handful of minutes passed before there was another knock at the door.

Wiping his hands dry, Johnny moved from the kitchen sink expecting to see Tony return, maybe something he'd forgotten to mention.

Johnny opened the door blurting out. "And what do you want now?"

To his amazement there stood Angela and Allie. Johnny noticed the look on Angela's face. Understandably she was taken aback by the crude remark.

"Sorry, my dear. I thought you were an old friend. I only meant what I said in jest."

"That's okay, Father. I understand." Angela paused for a second and only to ensure there were no unexpected interruptions in her evil plan, she asked the question.

"Are you expecting someone?"

"No, he just left. I thought it was him coming back."

Angela observed a look of embarrassment lingering over Johnny's face. He may have been embarrassed by the way he greeted her at the door, but all Angela cared about was one thing and one thing only.

The Father was quick to break the uncomfortable silence.

"How may I help?"

"Forgive me, Father, I don't wish to intrude on your day of rest, but I must speak with you."

On the outer appearance of it all, Angela made certain her plea sounded a little desperate, but if only he knew her true intent for the need to be alone and uninterrupted with Johnny was paramount. Everything Angela had ever done since meeting Johnny would come together today.

Angela had introduced herself to him a while back as a struggling single parent and with regular catch ups, had kept up that charade. She would only have to pretend for a little while longer.

And besides, how could Johnny refuse to help this young mother. He was in the business of understanding and support whilst Angela deceptively hid behind her true intent—that is, the business of evil and wrong-doing. She cleverly tugged at his emotions and caring nature as gracefully as a concert pianist played her piano.

This was turning out exactly as Angela had intended it to.

There was only one thing left to do.

"That's quite all right, come in. Can I fix you both a drink? A hot cup of tea maybe?"

Angela looked at Allie, got the acknowledgement she was seeking, and then replied accordingly.

"Thank you. That would be lovely."

"And how do you like your drinks?"

"We both have our teas with milk. No sugar, but a little more milky for Allie please."

"Make yourselves comfortable." Johnny directed the mother and daughter to the table before turning on the kettle.

As Angela and Allie were about to be seated in the kitchen, the spiritual forms of Sebastian and Lucifer entered the front of the church.

Pam had taken a moment out of her time to admire the stoup with all of its imperfections.

Lucifer was quick to signal to Sebastian and in an instant they made their way to where Pam was.

She got a tap on the shoulder.

Startled by the touch of fingers on her spiritual soul, she turned.

There they stood. Lucifer and Sebastian side by side.

Instantly frightened, her sight fixed on the devil. He was tall; her head was tilted back and out of the corner of her eye she could see Sebastian snarling in silence.

The presence of demons in a place of worship hit her like frosty wind on naked skin. The chill of terror ran through her core. In that moment Pam was able to react.

She gasped.

Very quickly, she understood the dimensions of her predicament. The two faces before her were no strangers to her. She quickly faced the reality; resistance was futile, and fighting back—she stood no chance.

She winced as Sebastian reached out and held onto her shoulder. The grip strong and hard, she was no match for the demonic General.

A chance meeting, spiritual forms of opposed sides.

She hesitantly asked, "What do you want with me?"

There was no answer to her question, instead Sebastian and Lucifer screamed at her ghostly presence. Their clicks and chants came out with ferocity which if directed to mortal man, would shake its soul to the very core.

Pam would never know the demonic Lord and his trusted General were both as surprised to run into her as she was to them, but at the end of their chance meeting, it was the demons which retained the element of surprise.

And in times of spiritual war there is no time for prisoners, only time for casualties. No demon ever refused the opportunity to rid the world of another heavenly soul.

The demons proceeded quickly.

Sebastian vibrated his head from side to side, so fast, his face now a blur. Lucifer continued to scream, high pitched shrieks, clicks and curses.

The demonic duo worked together and quickly to send Pam's soul back to its origins.

Pam was not going to get an answer to her question.

There was a quiver in her voice as she screamed for help. No-one was around to hear. She managed to get out a short cry, the brief shriek echoing off the church walls.

It fell on deaf ears.

Cries of mercy and help meant nothing to the demons.

Soon the yells stopped and the tears began as Pam faced the terrible truth.

There was no sympathy here as the demons attacked in their sinister ways as ferociously as lions on a fresh kill.

Pam went to scream again, maybe someone up above could hear, but if only. Her vocals, now paralysed with silence, the volume completely muted. She screamed some more, but heard nothing come out of her mouth.

It was useless. The screams stopped and were replaced with an eerie lull.

Pam stood there silently, intoxicated in fear.

Pam was in dire straits and there for the taking. There was no point in fighting back. The best she could do was prepare herself for the inevitable.

Pam looked down at the stoup which in that split second, blew as aggressive as any volcanic eruption. It was as if the Holy water was acting in violence against the presence of demonic beings. It burst out of its bowl not leaving a droplet behind. All traces of holy water sat in tiny puddles on the floor of the foyer.

There was no further movement in the spilt over blessed water.

Pam looked up, the outside of her spiritual entity paralysed and afraid, her internal psyche well aware of what was going on.

Pam stood there, unable to do anything, lifelessness in her spiritual body, unable to react in any way.

And how ironic that in her afterlife, Pam would get to experience for the first time, the sensation of feeling death approaching, for in her mortal existence, her heart attack hit her hard and fast. She never saw or sensed her living years come to an end.

With no further fight or signs of resistance, Pam felt the hand of Sebastian let go which left her dangling like a piece of meat on a butcher's hook.

Sebastian and Lucifer took their positions, their faces up close and personal with Pam's. With evil in their sinister voices, they communicated directly with her soul.

Time appeared to stretch out, every second feeling like twenty.

Pam trembled inside, petrified at the vision of having two demonic faces up close and personal. With every demonic scream, Pam felt her internals tremor with an intensity and magnitude off the Richter scale.

All she could manage was to brace herself for what was about to happen.

Pam could hear and see, but do absolutely nothing about it. Paralysed in the true sense, she now couldn't even lift a finger.

Frozen to the core, shivers running rampant up and down her spiritual spine, she waited for her demise.

She knew it, she could feel it - the end was near and she was powerless to change the outcome.

The devil wanted her gone. He let out his mighty yell. Sebastian followed immediately, shrieking and cursing.

For a few seconds beforehand there was an emptiness in Pam's eyes.

All was blacker than the void of outer space and then it happened. That eerie crack, her soul destroyed.

Pam was gone.

Pam vanished from the church foyer leaving no trace of ever having been there.

She was on her way in accordance to spiritual and heavenly law, the tiny moment of time between existing and re-appearing to be rehabilitated. The moment of transition appeared to stretch out for an eternity for Pam.

Firstly her world was dark, as black as black could be. A short moment afterwards, streaks of lightning flashed by her way as if she were standing in the middle of a terrible thunder storm. The cracks were sharp, the flashes of bright white light smashing close by, blinding and hauntingly loud.

A short moment later dark and silence.

The black intermixed with the streaks of white. Moments of terrifying blinding light interchanged with moments of still black. The pattern repeated itself over and over again.

Pam was petrified.

The experience appeared to last an eternity, but in reality went for only a few short minutes.

Pam then heard a sickening crunch, as if two cars had collided at full speed. The sound was short, sharp and metallic.

By the laws of heaven, all souls return to her sacred ground, be it by death, regardless of whether you are: a mortal, spirit, demonic or an angelic being. For a better term, all who die re-enter their existence in heaven.

This may have once been the law which existed in God's kingdom, but now, heaven was in complete chaos. The normal laws that once existed had fallen apart. The balance in heaven's harmony and loving nature had been upset with the invading demonic terrors and with it, heaven's laws had become topsy-turvy.

After her shock encounter with the devil and his loyal servant Sebastian, Pam appeared in a world foreign to her.

Pam knew the workings of heaven extremely well. After all, her duties involved rehabilitating spirits and souls and educating these spirits on the ways of God's kingdom. Its laws and the ways of rehabilitation were all part of what Pam did. She was a counsellor of sorts to those who had passed on.

This was her angelic-given destiny.

And because of this, Pam could cope with her recent trauma better than many. She was resilient enough to recover relatively quickly from an experience that would shock many other souls for weeks and months on end.

A bit more time and she'd be able to think a little clearer.

A roaring sound in the background, a yellowy light breaking up the darkness all around.

Pam took a moment longer to recompose herself and then stood. She rubbed at her eyes and massaged her forehead. Pam was suffering a pain likened to a terrible and throbbing migraine, far worse than anything she had ever experienced in her lifetime.

She continued to rub at it. With every passing second, the pain settled just a little.

Her eyes were blurred and a strange smell hit her spiritual senses with the sharpness of icy pepper.

Her smell and vision, being attacked from all angles.

She continued to rub at her head. It seemed to help.

Her agitated emotions slowly settled. Calming her spirit was the solution.

The rubbing turned into gentle massaging. Pam gently stroked her face and then ran her hands and arms over her entire torso. A gentle self-massage of sorts.

The pain in her head soon subsided and the blurriness in her vision soon returned to a crisp focus.

Although still irritating, the smell didn't bother her as it first had.

She was now able to take in the detail of her surroundings.

The sound, smell and sight of it all.

Although settled, at least as well as could be expected, Pam experienced a new sensation. It felt like she had goose bumps all over.

Something was terribly wrong, really wrong.

She felt out of place, every spiritual cell in her body was telling her so, and one thing was for certain. Whatever location she had been sent to, this was definitely not heaven.

Chapter Twenty-five
Demons at Work

Allie sat with her mother opposite the priest. She kept silent and allowed her mother to do all the talking.

Allie knew her part in this masquerade. There would be a time for her to intervene, but not yet. For now, Allie kept her mouth shut and played the dual role of a shy young girl and demon host.

Johnny had finished serving the hot drinks and sat himself down.

"So how may I help?" he asked.

Her mother appeared a little nervous. A short lived, uncomfortable silence lingered in the room, only to be broken by a mother's sigh.

Angela was playing for time and both Allie and Angela knew it.

"I wasn't sure who to turn to. It has been a difficult time for us."

Angela's opening statement got his attention. She paused for a moment longer to sip on her hot tea.

The subtle slurp was all anyone could hear. Angela then placed the hot cup carefully back on the table top, drawing out the moment a little longer before looking up to continue.

Angela's eyes had that appearance of being ashamed. She spoke with nervousness.

"Father, I have been running from my husband. He has a drinking problem."

Allie looked up as Johnny shifted his caring eyes off Angela to meet with hers. Johnny's gentle smile and supportive gaze was heartfelt. Allie responded with a cute shyness.

Allie quickly broke eye contact, shifting her head downward and away.

"Should the child be hearing this about her father?" asked Johnny.

"It's quite all right. Anything I say here today has already been spoken about with my daughter."

"Is this a situation of physical abuse?" asked Johnny.

"He never hit me, Father; never laid a hand on Allie. But the screaming matches. When he was sober he was tolerable. When he drank, we would shout the ceiling down."

Johnny, like many, did not like hearing what he was listening to. Johnny was none the wiser. There was no truth to this story, but this fairy tale had been delivered with a convincing deception.

With a stiff and angry hand, Johnny reached for his hot tea, but spilt a bit when lifting it to his mouth. Placing his cup back down, he got up to get a cloth from his kitchen sink. As he walked away, Allie looked at her mother.

Her mother flashed back a wink of her eye and a quaint smile. Allie replied with a quick smile before getting all serious again. Her role was to play the part of a shy young girl and that she did.

Johnny returned with his sponge and mopped up the spilt tea. He never saw the act between mother and daughter. He then put his sponge back on the kitchen sink and sat back down.

The time to reveal their true intent had not yet arrived and so mother and daughter were back to playing out their evil charade for a little longer.

"Sorry, Angela, now where were we?"

"Well, Father." Angela paused for a second or two. Angela delivered her closing summary with a combination of conviction, remorse and sorrow as if she had really lived the life of a wife of a long term and abusive alcoholic.

"There's not too much more to this. We lived in a house with a chronic alcoholic. Day to day, we lived with uncertainty, never knowing when the smallest of things would lead to the most violent of shouting matches."

Angela looked and fixed her eyes on her daughter.

"I finally had enough and left him."

There was a short silence before Angela continued with her well-rehearsed lie. Angela resumed the discussion with Johnny.

"This is why we shifted here. I had to put some distance between us and him."

"I see," remarked Johnny.

Allie's eyes met with Johnny's once again, a beautiful smile painted across her face.

Suddenly Angela and Allie sensed their presence.

They were not visible to anyone, not yet anyway, but Sebastian and Lucifer were definitely in the room standing nearby in their spiritual forms.

Allies eyes gazed upon Johnny and Johnny looked back with a caring sincerity.

In a flash everything changed.

Allies eyes suddenly rolled back, revealing only the whites of her eyeballs.

Johnny reacted as if he had been slapped in the face unexpectedly. It took a brief few seconds to process the events before him.

Unknown to Johnny, Allie was willingly allowing Lucifer to repossess her soul. It was that time again where their souls would meet and work side by side for the common demonic goal.

Thinking it was some sort of illness, Johnny turned to Angela and was about to ask the question of whether or not to seek medical attention, but before he could open his mouth, Angela intervened with a purpose-filled rudeness. She blurted the words at him as quick as a bullet.

"YOUR SOUL IS OURS."

At this point, Lucifer had completed his possession of Allie, her eyes returning to normality, but now the whites of Allie's eyeballs were a blood red.

With Allie's whole hearted acceptance, Lucifer was now the driver of Allie's body.

A demon's voice boomed out of the young female child. It screamed at the priest with high shrieks and clicks. Unbeknown to Johnny, Lucifer was cursing the priest in his native hell-bound language.

Johnny reacted apprehensively and defensively, his years of karate training kicking in. He stood and backed off cautiously, never lifting his look off his two female guests.

Angela got up and walked steadily towards the Father, who was backed into the corner of the rear wall of the church's kitchen/office. Allie got up out of her seat to follow behind her mother.

"Don't you see?" Angela asked.

"It is time you came with us." Angela added.

Allie (Lucifer) cursed again in her language of shrieks and clicks. It hit Johnny like venom from a deadly snake bite. Johnny shivered uncontrollably, his body temperature unable to maintain warmth needed for human survival.

Sebastian looked upon Johnny from the spiritual world. The two had met in battle in the old gothic cathedral of Cologne and Sebastian had paid the price for his defeat back then.

"What goes around, comes around," Sebastian spoke from his spiritual world. "I suffered back then, let him suffer now," he yelled from his spiritual domain.

All in the room heard Sebastian bar Johnny.

Every fibre of Johnny's soul was yelling fight or flight. Leaving the scene was not easy; defending himself was his only option.

Johnny instinctively put up his guard, he was prepared to punch and kick his way out if he had to.

Angela stopped. Three metres of empty space was all that stood between her and Johnny.

For now, Johnny remained in his corner. With his back hard up against the church wall. If he was going to be attacked then it would be from front on.

An eerie silence filled the air. Angela allowed Allie to step forward.

The young child presented with bloodiness in her eyes and fire in her voice.

She cursed at the priest again. "YOUR SOUL IS OURS."

Johnny was a fighter before he was a priest. Johnny looked back at his female visitors with a look he would give an opponent in a competition fight. The time for counselling and spiritual guidance was well and truly over.

Johnny took to the ready. His knees slightly bent and feet firmly on the ground, staggered slightly and positioned shoulder width apart. Whether it be to lunge forward or dodge and parry. Whatever the occasion called for, he would defend himself or attack vigorously, calling upon his many years of dedicated martial arts training.

Suddenly, Allie yelled with an intensity that blew out the back windows of the church.

The sound was deafening and Johnny reacted instinctively, dropping his guard and dropping his head, simultaneously raising his flattened hands in an effort to cover his ears and protect his eardrums from the deafening boom.

In that instant of vulnerability, Angela made her move and restrained Johnny, thrusting forward, using her strength and moving momentum to pin Johnny hard up against the rear wall of the church.

Allie moved in quickly, standing only a few inches apart from her priestly victim.

Her small stature looked up at Johnny as she let out another mighty yell.

The attack was swift. Johnny never saw it coming, never dodged, parried or threw out a punch. The only thing he managed to do was drop his guard and fall victim to the demonic cursing and screaming. He stood there as Pam had only moments before, paralysed and unable to lift a finger.

The communication in the room was now between Lucifer and Johnny's soul. Sebastian snarled and screamed from his spiritual domain and Lucifer did the same from his physical world.

Johnny's soul was taking a battering. Being attacked from two different dimensions, from two different realms—but both had the same intentions.

It didn't take long before Johnny could feel his life force drain. With every scream and every curse, the spirit weakened.

The attack swift and violating. The curses felt down deep in Johnny's core as if someone had reached down and grabbed hold of his spine, shaking it violently from one side to the next.

The rattling inside lasted a minute or two until Johnny's eyeballs rolled.

Totally helpless, the cracking and destruction of Johnny's soul was imminent.

A sharp crack sounded out. It could only mean one thing.

The four demonic friends celebrated their victory soon after.

~ * ~

In the spiritual plane, Archangels Michael, Gabriel and the angel Raphael had gathered in a quiet corner in the upper levels of heaven.

An emergency meeting of sorts.

Concerning to the angelic trio, news had travelled fast.

Johnny's mortal physical body and loving spiritual soul no longer lived together in harmony. The clergyman's body now housed the spirit of a demon General who went by the name of Sebastian.

Johnny's spirit had recently been vacated in preparation for demonic possession. In time, Johnny's body would begin the slow process of necrosis like the poor souls who suffered with Sebastian's last rampage in the cities of Germany.

Sebastian was in physical form back then, but it didn't matter. Whether the demon lived in physical state or spiritual state, the consequences of possession remained the same, for no mortal body can live without its soul.

It is simply a shell and like back then, at a time when Sebastian utilised his victims' bodies to move around the cities of Germany incognito, he would have free reign to do what he liked using Johnny's body as a vehicle. He would work that body like a puppeteer works his puppet, the only difference being Sebastian's spiritual presence would control his 'puppet' from the inside of a shell of a body.

The angelic trio were all aware of Sebastian's doing on Earth, but only Archangel Michael knew a little more than the rest of the angels.

"And one more thing," added Michael.

Michael had spent recent times searching frantically for it and unfortunately the time had come to be the bearer of further bad news.

"I have looked high and low, my friends. I am at a total loss." Michael looked down from the upper level of heaven. He stared at many a demon wandering freely on the ground that was once a place that spirit and angel wondered freely.

This was his heaven, his home, and he was sick of seeing the invading terrors below him.

How much more damage can they do? Archangel Michael was determined. The time to bring this war to an end was near, but for now, all he could manage was a stare at the grounds below.

He spoke with a sadness in his voice and anger in his eyes as he informed his angelic friends. The news was not good.

"My friends, I cannot find her," he announced, still looking down.

Michael then raised his head. His eyes met with a puzzled look from both Gabriel and Raphael.

"I do not know what those demons have done with her, but Pam's spirit is nowhere to be found."

Chapter Twenty-six
A Different Place

Pam looked around. She struggled to make sense of her new surroundings. Her mind a clouded mess, as if she were hung over after a heavy night on whiskey. There she stood in a confused daze, looking out into the vastness of unfamiliarity.

On this different type of spiritual land, Pam stood for quite some time. Her migraine-like pain had dulled to a niggly ache some time ago. Her vision had returned to a clear crisp focus back then as well, but her ability to comprehend and to understand was suppressed.

Death was traumatising even to those who lived in the after-life. Apart from time, comfort and nurturing were the key ingredients to regaining one's identity. This was the process known as spiritual rehabilitation.

However, Pam now stood on a foreign land, isolated from all her friends and loved ones. Not an angel or spirit in sight.

This was not her heaven.

This is not what it is supposed to be, she thought to herself. *Where are my counsellors, my spirits, my angelic friends?* she questioned.

Pam had retained the memory of her demonic torture. For now, that didn't bother her so much, yet the absence of due process of her own rehabilitation did.

Something was amiss.

And one thing was for certain. She needn't have clarity in her thinking to realise she'd have to pull through this one completely on her own.

All of this was too overwhelming and Pam hadn't the energy to stand any longer. The moment had come to give in to the unfamiliarity of it all.

Pam would have gracefully lowered herself on the floor, legs comfortably crossed, but with her body drained, she simply collapsed in a heap. She hit the ground with a solid thud.

Lying on her side, her posture slouched over as if she were hunchbacked, she couldn't even muster up the strength to straighten out her spiritual spine.

Attacked on all three fronts; she was physically, spiritually and mentally drained. Her only choice was to work on a meditative type of calming. Steadying breaths, thinking of nothing but peace and calm.

She mustered up her last ounce of energy to roll on her back. From there, she closed her eyes and dozed off.

~ * ~

Pam awoke.

She felt as though a few blissful hours had past. If only she had known it had been several days, not that time mattered much in this different place. Either way, the long restful sleep had helped.

Pam raised her open palms to her face. She could feel the warmth of the glow within her emanating out like the sun's rays. Her spiritual life force had returned.

Over the course of Pam's hibernation, her strength and vitality had filled her soul and although not quite one hundred percent, she was good enough to get up and go.

She spoke the self-talk out aloud and it was said with a determination in her inner voice. *Get it together, Pam; it's up to you now.*

Pam stood up with the sluggishness of drunkenness. She consciously put the effort in to steady herself. It was hard going. For the longest moment, she swayed side to side as if she were balancing on a tight rope. Never enough to topple over, but enough to look like a toddler taking its first steps.

It didn't take too long before the sways slowly drifted away, allowing Pam to steady her stance.

Not convinced, however, she played around with a few steps back and forth and repeated it one more time for assurance. The mechanics of taking a walk soon returned to normality.

Pam was virtually freed of the mental anguish which once engulfed her. The ability to think and move without further hindrance was a blessing. Now, the moment had finally arrived. For the first time, Pam could finally appreciate and take in all that was around her.

Her mind no longer clouded and muddled, her thinking clearer, her processing much more rational and methodical, she looked at her new surroundings with the innocence of a child. The sight before her was scarily fresh and new, its landscape massive, stretching wide and far.

Directly in front of her were fiery waves crashing upon the shoreline, much like that of an ocean. This sea was different; unlike any Pam had ever seen before. Yellowy orange with fire that roared off its undulating surface. They rolled in one after the other, the flames crashed into the ground several metres in front of her and then retreated to its massive origin. Time and time again, the fire rolled in with a mighty crackle and retreated almost silently.

With every crash on its shoreline, the radiant heat pulsated forth with an intense warmth.

The fiery glow left her standing with knots in her abdominal area, crunching and squeezing her spiritual insides. Warm it was, comforting it wasn't.

The fiery ocean went off to the horizon for as far as the eye could see, its yellowy light competing with the blackness of the terrain in the vast distance until at its farthest point, all Pam could make out was a complete wall of black.

A full three hundred and sixty degree view of her landscape was in order, but she would take it in one piece at a time.

Pam turned a quarter circle, shifting her eyes away from the fiery ocean. The wide and lengthy ravine to her side stretched to the distance like a giant 'Y,' the ravine's length dissected much of the grounds to the immediate right of her.

She continued turning right and back around, her eye following the ravine back to where it appeared to start.

Where the ravine came to end, the land from here was simply dark and barren. As plain as it comes, not a rock or undulation, as if it had been levelled flat, doused with petroleum, lit, allowed to burn and then fizzle out, leaving behind its charred remains.

The burnt surface ran for the length of a few football fields until it connected with the base of a large, mound-like structure.

Even from as far back as Pam was, at about mid-way up the hill, she noticed a change in the appearance of the ambient light. The typical yellowy glow that occupied much of this land at this point intermixed with a massive source of white light. The whiteness appeared soft and billowy, like giant clouds.

Even at this great separation, Pam recognised God's light in an instant and the light appeared to recognise her.

Suddenly there was a distinct change in the white light's characteristic as it danced around like an excited puppy, moving with sharp shifts to its right and left.

The light somehow knew one of its own, that Pam was in need of its healing properties.

It shone mid-height around the hilly face, putting a glowing perspective on the steep, hilly gradient.

Pam took her first steps towards it. She'd have to get closer to the light. That she knew for sure.

She would undertake the lengthy task and follow the ravine's path until she got to barren land. From there she would be closer to the hillside, in a better position to assess her personal situation.

She walked alongside the ravine. The walk was long and time consuming.

Still in the mode of recovering, her legs didn't appear to work as efficiently as she had hoped for. Pam walked her chosen path a slow and steady pace.

All normality would return in time, Pam was certain of this, but for now, Pam persevered, doing the best with what she had available to her.

It took some time but she was considerably closer now. Close enough to get a clearer panoramic view of the hillside before her. It ran the width of the valley.

She ran her tired eyes up the hilly face, moving her head slightly to the left and right. Mapping out what would become the best path to take. The only way around it was to go up and over it. Pam could see no other way.

She found a pathway; narrow, steep, which allowed for a manageable climb. She followed it with her eyes, ensuring the path reached the upper edge face. It ran all the way up to what appeared like a volcanic lip. It was way up high above the valley floor below.

She knew what path to take; she just had to get there.

Pam continued with her walking, still following the ravine's path towards the hill face. It was hard going.

She sighed heavily and then steadied her breathing.

A meditative-like deep breath in and then out. In and out. In and then out.

The pungent smell of fire combined with brimstone still biting at her senses, her abdomen still in knots.

With eyes fixed on the hill face before her, Pam noticed a sudden change in the white light. It changed from its agitated shifts to one of seeking out.

It began to descend from mid-height and reached out to Pam.

Streams of light broke off from the massive billowy light source. Bright, skinny fingers flowed downwardly and when it got to the valley floor, floated above and along the barren surface.

It shone its soft light on the charred surface below as it stretched out its reach; five thin wavy beams.

It made its way to Pam as Pam walked her way towards it.

She was not afraid.

The heavenly light that occupied this land sought to heal the injuries of one of God's children.

In a short time, the fingers of white glow wrapped their healing source around Pam and Pam welcomed its presence with open arms. She stretched her body as far and as wide as it would go, the white light wrapping itself around her like a boa constrictor.

It was soothing, comforting, protective, something she should have had a long time ago, as per the normal process of rehabilitation. Well overdue, Pam welcomed whatever nurturing she could get from the light source.

Pam stood tall and gently shut her eyes, exposing every square centimetre of her being to this loving light.

With clearer thinking came clarity.

The reality then hit like an unexpected slap to the face. Pam's eyes snapped open.

She had been told of this place. It was common knowledge amongst those who walked in God's presence.

It all made sense now; the fiery ocean, the barren land, the pungent smell of brimstone and God's Light, shining because of what Johnny and Tony had accomplished a long time ago.

How they ventured deep into hell to lay down God's light in order to disrupt all that serves the demonic master. The pieces to her mystery jigsaw puzzle came rushing to her in the time it took to open her eyes.

She was in Hell Central.

As much as Pam enjoyed bathing in the soothing light, the sudden daunting reality of moving onward was a must. She had to get out of this place and fast.

Pam made her move and somehow the light knew. The fingers of light retracted slowly, making their way back towards where they had originated.

It was okay, she was feeling much better having had the experience.

The fingers led the way, retreating along the ravine's path. Pam followed at her own pace, the light retracting far quicker than Pam could manage to walk.

Very quickly there was some distance put between her and the light, yet the light was still leading her.

Then, as the thought of it rushed through her mind, she shivered with fear.

The situation had not been given any consideration up until now.

Pam stopped.

What if she was not alone?

She looked around cautiously in fear of demonic presence. She scanned every bit of surface carefully, but she could not see another being. She looked to the dark skies in search of winged demon. The sky as barren as the ground below her. A welcome relief, the world before her, completely desolate.

Pam resumed her slow and steady pace.

By this time, the whiteness of the light had put considerable distance between Pam and it.

Up ahead, Pam noticed the change in God's light. It changed as quickly as the flick of a switch. It went from being soft and billowy to one of focussed, like that of a spot light.

It concentrated its downward beam on a large standalone rock on the outer edge of the ravine. This solitary structure stood where the ravine ended (or where it began—dependant on where you were walking from).

Somehow Pam instinctively knew. The light wanted her there and Pam was keen to oblige.

With every tiring step, Pam drew closer to it.

God's light continued to beam down, its only interest to put focus on this solitary rock and the immediate area around it.

Pam was close by.

The ravine's end and this single rock were only a small street block away.

She could now see it. There was movement up ahead, another soul now bathed in God's light.

A soothing moan filled the air.

A pair of legs sticking out from behind the rock. Pam saw the gentle movement of legs until a sudden shift in the white light from above changed from one solid beam to that of stretched out fingers.

Its wavy beams danced around, above and behind the rock.

Pam made a direct and hurried walk towards the ravine's edge.

She was almost there when the body behind the rock stood and collapsed almost immediately. The injured soul could not maintain an upright position.

The white light did its best to help, but this poor soul was too drained to even stand.

Pam approached the rock a bit more cautiously.

The body stood again, maintained its balance for a few more seconds and collapsed.

Pam heard the crashing thud.

Pam instantly ran towards it. She mustered up all her energy, taking her slow and steady stroll to a mid-paced run.

"Johnny!" She couldn't keep the panic from her voice.

"Johnny, are you okay?" She bent over to help him on his feet, but the best she could manage was to sit him on the barren floor, upright with back leaning against the rock.

Johnny looked up to Pam. The world inside his mind was delusional and distraught, but he at least had the common sense to know who was standing before him.

With sympathetic eyes, he looked up to a female he had known all his life.

Johnny's eyes squinted, his body slumped and weak, his voice faint and gravelly. The first words spoken to Pam were a straight forward question.

Pam replied with a frown that instantly filled her face. She shrugged her shoulders, quickly followed with a subtle head movement, left and right, nodding back her 'I don't know why?'

How does one respond when asked, "If there is a God then why did he desert me?"

Chapter Twenty-seven
Dream Message

Tony had made peace with his family home, but there was a significant period in his young life where he didn't want anything to do with or go anywhere near the property.

The memories of a mother and father having passed on so early in his childhood were unbearable to him. This family home was the hurtful link which always bought back the reminders.

So he distanced himself, had nothing to do with the home until the day came when on his twenty fifth birthday, his grandfather would tell Tony the history behind the acquisition of the family property.

In particular what his father, Charlie, had sacrificed to win back the love of his mother, Mary.

This home gave hope to Mary.

It offered her security and an opportunity to rekindle a relationship with a husband who abandoned his family at a time when their only son was a little older than newborn.

Charlie couldn't cope with the pressures of being a young father and left without a trace, to work in the outback gas fields, leaving Mary behind to live the life of a lonely wife and single mother.

Never knowing why, Mary understandably suffered with anxiety and depression, but she eventually pulled through because of her natural inner strength, along with the support of a loving and understanding family.

When Mary would fall, then her mother Pam, father Arthur and brothers Jack and Chris would always be there in her hour of need.

But it was this point that had to hit its mark and as a twenty fifth birthday present, Arthur would deliver this message to his young grandson in the best way he knew how.

It wasn't easy, but Tony needed to know. He needed to understand there was a time in his infant life where his father abandoned him and consequently a time where his father came back to re-establish the love of his wife and child.

Charlie wanted nothing more than to have his family together again as it always should have been and with that firm belief, fought to win back the love of his estranged wife.

Tony would come to know all this only at his twenty fifth year. Come to know that his father bought the family home, unconditionally putting it in Mary's name.

This was her insurance. She would have a home to call her own if the relationship didn't work out.

But things couldn't have been better.

Charlie and Mary's love grew for one another and the three of them became a family again.

For the first time in twenty five years, Tony heard the whole truth. One of abandonment and return, of struggles and hardships, of love and of the importance of togetherness.

This was Tony's history and somehow knowing this made it bearable to eventually return to his childhood home.

With this new found knowledge, Tony ultimately moved out from his grandfather's place to live by himself. He moved back into his family home.

It was always there waiting for him.

And besides, relatives and friends were never too far away, but this wasn't ever a concern for Tony, for he was okay with his new found solitude.

And tonight, there was nothing left to do, but watch the mid-evening programming.

All alone, stretched out on his couch, Tony's eye's struggled to stay open.

Tired; an early night's sleep was in order. Tony turned the television off and made his way to the bathroom before retiring to his bed.

He was not alone.

In the spiritual world were his mother and father.

Mary spoke, "We must warn him," As she looked at her husband with anxious eyes.

"The news of Johnny's death is spreading through the heavens like a forest fire," she added. "He needs to know what happened to Johnny," she said frantically.

"I fear they will come after our Tony next," added Charlie. Charlie's ghostly presence stood over his son like a president's bodyguard.

There was only one thing they could do and trust that when Tony came to the time to face off with those demons, then in his time of need, all the 'dots would connect.'

It would be Mary who would lead the way. Her message, her warning, would be communicated through dreams.

It was mid-evening Monday night, earlier than the usual eleven pm bedtime ritual. Tony set his head into the pillow. The bedside light was switched off and it wasn't long before Tony went into deep sleep.

Mary knew she had to set the scene, but it would be Tony who would have to steer the way and experience the emotions.

After all, this was his dream, and unbeknown to Tony, his mother was nearby to play the part of a 'spiritual dream guide.'

So Tony dreamed his dream.

~ * ~

I stood alone in an empty parking lot.

Not a single soul in sight.

And to the front of me, bitumen with white marked lines for as far as the eye could see. I couldn't possibly count all the spaces before me, but at a broad guess, a place set for many hundreds upon hundreds of car parks.

Behind me, and only a small distance away was a giant wall. A shade of grey and as smooth as glass.

I ran my eyes upwardly, but there was no ending to it. It went up and up and up. I returned my gaze to street level and looked left and right and yet there were no edges. This wall was as high as it was wide.

I looked for a door, an opening, a rear exit, but there was nothing. Whatever this place, this wall marked one end of it.

There was no turning back, just moving forward, but not just yet.

Why the need for so many parking spaces?

I looked around me to find the answer and I could not.

I wasn't in a shopping district where the malls and colourful shops were alive with the hustle and bustle of city shoppers, nor near an industrial estate where chimney stacks billow out toxic fumes into the atmosphere and the sound of production and manufacturing are banging about for the workers to hear.

There was nothing of the sort, just an empty parking lot with me in it for company.

There had to be something more to this and the answer lay somewhere in front of me.

Something else caught my attention off into the distant horizon.

I could see them coming, you'd have to be blind not to!

Great, dark grey thunder clouds gulped up the sky before me.

I felt time go fast forward and in an instant I felt I was in the middle of a terrible storm, unlike any I had ever experienced in all my days on Earth.

The heavy dark clouds pushed forward and before I knew it, they were above me and still advancing. They wanted to travel beyond the giant wall, but the wall face behind me stopped any further movement.

The grey wall maintained its height and integrity and the dark clouds settled into position next to it.

The threat up above was enormous and with no exit to the rear of me, and darkness all above, I was trapped, surrounded by my own makeshift dream jail in colours of shades of grey.

I waited for the downpour, for the lightning, for the hail. The formation above could have struck at me with all three at once if it wanted to, but it didn't.

This was my dream. I knew the cloud above to be inanimate and yet deep inside, I felt in some ways that this thing was a living entity with sinister intents.

That this gloominess that hung above in the sky was waiting for the opportunity to hurt me.

For the longest time, or so it appeared to me, I stared at it and the swollen blackness looked back down at me. I feared the extreme and waited for anything to come hurling down from above.

I stood at the ready. I would dodge, run or dive if I had to.

I would not go down without a fight.

This cloud had the power to hurt me, maybe kill me, if it chose to do so and I suspected that it would happen anytime soon.

But my suspicions were wrong. I eventually grew tired of its empty threats and moved onward.

I only took a few steps and felt time thrust forward again as if I was walking in fast motion.

When I came to a stop I could see it.

A single solitary structure in front of me.

Wait a minute, I knew this building.

It was a church, but not like any church. This was Johnny's church.

I saw the door open ajar, and suddenly, a single arm reached out, waving me in.

It was waving at me sort of sluggishly, but never-the-less, the message was clear. The arm was telling me to get inside.

I'd like to say it was Johnny behind the door, but the truth be known, I couldn't tell for certain.

I walked towards the door.

For every step I took, I fast forwarded three, like I was on some sort of video movie and the controller was fast forwarding me bit by little bit.

It felt strange, every time the fast forwarding stopped I had to regain my focus and steady my step only for me to be fast forwarded again.

By the time I got to the church doors, thankfully the time lapsing stopped, but unfortunately, so did the waving arm.

It no longer appeared from behind the wood.

I stalled for time.

In a way I hoped it would come back out and wave me back in, but it never re-appeared so I gave up on waiting for it, but I also hesitated on stepping in.

Up close and personal, the church appeared bigger than how I remembered it.

I wasn't a small man, height ran in my family.

Me, I stood a little over six foot and with a strong jump, I could reach the door seal up above. I know because I had done so previously.

On one of my many visits to see my friend, Johnny, I couldn't resist the temptation to try and touch the top of the church's door seal and as soon as I told Johnny, neither could he.

On that afternoon, don't ask me why, but in a moment of fun and games, we both jumped in the front of a church door, making a silly competition out of it and we eventually both got to do what we set out to do.

The meaningless antics friends get up to when no one is watching!

But now, the doors were four, maybe five times my size. I would need an elevator to reach the top.

I ran my eyes up. The dimensions before me were largely exaggerated. Not only the door, but the steeples, the church windows, the crucifix; the whole package. This church was made out to me in my mind's eye to be larger than life, but one thing was for certain, this was definitely Johnny's cathedral.

Suddenly, my attention was broken by a loud thud.

The arm now bringing me a message from the other side of the door.

It, or whoever the arm belonged to, wanted me inside.

It knocked again, a single thud, hard and loud.

I complied, but I did not let the church door touch me, the door ajar enough for me to squeeze my body through side-on.

I was inside now and what I saw sent a shiver through my spine.

Car parking bays for as far as the eye could see, bitumen stretched to the horizon separated by evenly spaced white lines.

I looked behind me, I wanted to get out of this place, but the wooded church door quickly transformed before my eyes. It was a light grey wall again, much like the one I left behind at the start of my dream.

Before my very eyes and in the space of a few heartbeats, inside a church building quickly transformed into an outside car park.

In an instant, I realised I was back to where I had started.

This time I ran. I didn't stop to think about it, I just ran.

My stride was long, my pace fast. I ran across car park space after car park space so quickly, the white lines and dark grey bitumen became one. The car park lanes and their white lines of separation were to my moving body, a blurry mess.

I didn't worry about my fuzzy world around me, I simply enjoyed running like a cheetah on the hunt.

I could see it again. The church building way up ahead. It looked no bigger than a coin, but with my speed, I'd make the distance up fast.

The church grew in size as I drew closer to it.

I ran and I ran and I ran.

Only a short distance away, I was stopped in my tracks.

I skidded to a halt in awe of the vision before me.

This was Johnny's church again, the doors how I remembered them, not exaggerated, not out of proportion- just right.

A man and woman standing with their backs to me. Specifically, a bride and groom. Her with her long white gown trailing down and toward me. He, with his neatly pressed black suit, not a crinkle in its material.

They kept their backs to me and I did the only thing I knew to do.

I called out to them, "Hey, You There!"

They turned their heads. I watched this moment as if I were watching it in slow motion.

Up ahead, she stood to my right, him to my left. Their heads turned and if for the smallest time, when the bride's eyes met with the groom's, they paused for the briefest of moments to enjoy each other's smile.

My eyes wide opened with excitement now, I couldn't wait for them to turn around.

It was them!

Mum and Dad were at the church door. Dad never looked around but kept his loving eyes on his bride. Mum, however, shifted to face me, body and all.

She smiled her tender love for me and then quickly turned her back on me to face the church's entrance.

I wanted so much more but that was all Mum gave me.

Dad opened the church door a little wider and let Mum walk in first.

I called out to them.

"STOP!"

I didn't want to lose them. Not again... Not now... Not ever!

So close yet so far.

I waited for them to listen to me, but they would not.

I'm ignored.

Their one and only son and I'm ignored.

I cannot begin to tell you how that felt.

I was left with little choice but to watch Mum disappear behind the church door, her bridal dress quickly trailed. She had long disappeared from view, but I still saw her bridal gown material of white snaking its way along the ground.

Dad waited until the dress had fully disappeared and then and only at that point, turned to look at me for the first time.

A full turn, face to face, man to man... father to son.

I was a trembling mess inside. More nervous than I had ever been.

I looked at him and he at me.

We caught each other's smile, be it ever so briefly, and then suddenly, Dad about faced as if he were given army marching orders. He walked through the church's entrance, never looking back at me again.

Before I knew it, he was gone as well.

I stood there unable to breathe. I was at a loss to think my own parents wouldn't spend a little more time with me, but before I could give this further thought, a solitary arm re-appeared from behind the door, once again waving me closer.

I so wanted to be with them, but something inside me, my gut feeling, forced me to tread carefully.

I felt emotions of caution vibrate through every fibre of my body.

I walked steadily towards the door. Each step I took towards the wooded structure had it grow in size again. By the time I reached it, the door was out of proportion again, reaching three stories high, maybe four.

I didn't hesitate this time and walked in right after my parents. I braced myself to be thrust back to where I had started my dream, but instead found my Mum and Dad at the front altar.

Johnny is their priest, marrying the young couple on their special day.

I saw no crowd, no family; only Mum and Dad, hand in hand and Johnny performing his priestly duties.

I couldn't hear what he said initially, but there was no mistaking what he was doing.

I stopped to watch the service in silence. I did not wish to intrude on their special moment.

The sound slowly turned up.

I heard the voice of my friend as he preached his words on the meaning of holy matrimony.

It gradually got louder and louder, like someone turning up the knob on the stereo sound system. Soon the voices were pitching at their normal audio levels.

I listened to his traditional words spoken at such times.

"To honour and obey; in sickness and in health." We all know the words, but suddenly, something was very wrong with the sound again.

It's quickly became faint again. It was weak and fragile as if Johnny was on his dying breath, calling out for his last opportunity for help.

It's so unlike Johnny, he's as strong and as healthy as they make them.

The altar suddenly disappeared as did my mother and father.

I was left at one end of the church aisle, staring into the eyes of Johnny, my friend. We were only a handful of metres apart with nothing in between us except a church aisle.

We were standing face to face looking at each other as best friends do.

The look was short lived.

I watched him fall to the floor as if someone suddenly sucked out every bit of life force. His eyes were open, but there was a scary emptiness to them. Nothingness, almost soulless stares back at me.

He looked to me for help, but something was holding me back. I didn't want to rush to his aid, I wasn't sure why, but it was this gut instinct again.

I noticed the room go gloomy, another shade of grey.

Suddenly, Johnny exploded before me.

I reacted instinctively.

My head turned left and I raised my right forearm as I looked away and shielded my eyes from the blood and bodily spatterings.

I was afraid to look out, but look I must.

I slowly lowered my arm and returned my gaze to the front.

The blood and guts were gone and so was Johnny.

Two others now stood before me.

I instantly recognised one to be the devil.

He stood tall and as the scriptures described him. A solid build, red skinned with a pointy tail and small horns protruding from his head. There was no mistaking the ruler from hell.

Next to him, a demon of some sort. He carried some importance; he must have because Lucifer had his arms around him, protecting him like a father to a child.

They both looked at me with such ferocity.

Suddenly, Lucifer's face interchanged with Johnny's. One moment Johnny's face was superimposed on the devil's, the next vice versa.

Johnny's face smiled at me, but when the change occurred—when the devil's face placed itself back on Johnny's head, it looked back at me with a thriving threat.

The superimposing went back and forth; back and forth with Johnny's time becoming shorter and short lived until all I could see was the look of the devil.

The exchanging faces no longer occurred; I only saw the devil and his demon companion and the looks I got back were more concerning than ever.

Another change, as sudden as that!

The devil clothed, dressed as a clergyman, wearing the exact clothes Johnny wore before. The body was Johnny's, the face was definitely not.

Red skinned and horned, it's evil eyes stared back at me once again.

I didn't know whether to be angry, scared, concerned for my friend or all three at once.

Then for the moment I forget about the mixed emotions bubbling within me. I looked with a curiosity at the demon standing next to Lucifer. There was something in his manner, something in his looks that were vaguely familiar to me. There was something about this creature that played on my memory strings but I struggled to piece it altogether.

I simply looked at it and it snarled back at me.

My curious glance was broken suddenly by the addition of a vicious growl from the Devil. They yelled their hellish message to me in unison.

It came to me with changing pitch, high and low tones, screeches, yells and screams.

It was a language, but none that I had ever heard before, or had I?

Once again, a sense of familiarity washed over me. Had I seen this all before, had I heard this all before, but either way, I was never given the time to thoroughly think it through.

The devil remained in his clergyman's attire, with his sinister companion by his side.

Their cursing and snarling suddenly came to an end.

A few seconds of silence, their eyes locked with mine.

In unison, they took their steps towards me.

I knew my life to be in danger.

My need for self-preservation kicked in.

I didn't want to be here anymore.

TONY'S EYES SNAPPED OPEN!

Awake and in complete darkness, Tony frantically searched for his bedside light, his arm instinctively reaching out to find the switch in the dark. He missed once, twice and on his third attempt brought light into his bedroom.

The time on his alarm clock read three twenty-seven am.

Tony sat up.

His throat felt like sandpaper, his chest heaved with heavy nervous breaths. He needed a drink of water, but before he got up, he sat on the edge of the bed, steadying his thumping heart.

In the spiritual world, Mary turned to her husband.

"Do you think that was enough?" she asked hesitantly. "Will he get the point?"

Charlie took a moment and carefully planned out his reply. He didn't want to worry Mary any more than she was. He held his wife close and looked her lovingly in the eyes. His words came out soft and calm.

"When Tony and Johnny came out of battle with Sebastian at the gothic cathedral, we gave him a gift to remember, but took away their anguish. You and I made sure that Tony and Johnny would not be emotionally scarred for having fought one of Lucifer's demons in a holy place of worship."

"I remember," she said.

"Through our actions back then and with a little bit of time, his memory of his encounter with Sebastian may be a little vague, perhaps hazy, but it is there, deep inside his memory banks," said Charlie. "He is a spiritually connected young man. He needs to take your dream message and dig deeper, reach down deep inside. If he can manage that then all that he had experienced in the church tower fighting Sebastian, all of those terrible memories that we pushed into the recesses of his mind—they will come flooding back in an instant. Then I am certain Tony will make the connection. Linking his past experiences with your dream message will simply occur naturally."

Mary couldn't hide her worried looks. "I can only hope this serves its purpose when the time is right," she said.

Charlie paused to look at his son who had only just returned to his bedroom with a glass of water in his trembling hands.

Tony sat at his bed sipping on his water. His mother went over to sit by his side. If she couldn't hold him, she would be as close by to him.

Charlie looked at the ghostly presence of Mary who was looking over to her son. It was heart felt and yet bittersweet. It was moments like these that stirred a type of anger in Charlie for a father should be there to protect his children from harm.

And the reality of it all was that no plan ever had a one hundred percent certainty to it. The unexpected was always a given possibility and in spirit, their ability to help had limitations.

Charlie left the room. He would leave Mary sitting by her son.

As Charlie walked the passageway alone, he couldn't help but wonder.

For the time being, had they done enough?

Chapter Twenty-eight
Calling All Souls-Part I

As they walked together, Michael listened to the conversation between Archangel Gabriel and Madame Liz.

For many minutes, Michael had not uttered a single word.

Suddenly, Liz felt her psychic energy surge. It sent a jolt, a type of electric shock, through her spiritual body and she reacted by stopping in mid-sentence and mid-stride as if she were snap frozen. Every nerve impulse deep within her psyche was screaming out to her. Liz quickly realised that this was a matter of urgency.

Deadly silent, Madame Liz fixed her gaze on one of the warrior class angels. The two archangels took a step or two farther before they realised. The archangels then turned and looked back at Liz's unexpected reaction with curiosity.

In her afterlife, Madame Liz still retained her special gift. It was now time to help a friend in need in the spiritual world.

Liz walked closer to Archangel Michael, putting her comforting arm on his shoulder. She could feel it, it was bubbling inside him ready to explode. Up until now, she never would have thought it. He did a good job hiding his troubles from his fellow spiritual beings, but now there was no mistaking it, he was a dear friend in need of her guidance.

"What is it, Michael? I sense something different. Angels give me a feel good emotion filled with inner peace and calm, but there is something stirring within you that makes me experience quite the opposite."

A comfortable silence lingered in the air.

Liz rubbed Michael's shoulder as if to say we are here for you, as if to reiterate SHE was there for HIM.

"What is it, my friend?" Archangel Gabriel must have sensed it as well. Michael was finding it harder to hide what he had held deep within for so long.

Down below, on the lower grounds of heaven, demon soldiers were unruly, with infighting and quarrelling a common occurrence.

Archangel Michael was the first to look down and then Archangel Gabriel and Madame Liz shifted their vision from their upper level heavenly haven to down below. They all observed the disruptive behaviour on heaven's lower grounds.

After an uncomfortable and brief pause, Liz was the only one who looked back up. The archangels kept their eyes fixed on the demonic presence spread throughout heaven's land.

"Michael, we all have our breaking points and angels are no exceptions. There is something troubling you. I can feel it," stated Liz.

Michael and Gabriel both remained attentive to the growls and hisses rising up from below. Demonic screeches and screaming were echoing from the far corners of heaven's grounds, pulsating upwardly for the heavenly population to hear.

The demonic chatter appeared more aggressive in recent times. For most of the part, the demons used to converse with one another, but in more recent times, they appeared to demand of each other, shout to one another. Many a time, this led to pushing and shoving, the behaviour not unlike pack animals fighting for their alpha status.

Sometimes the demonic disputes ended as quickly as they started, the lesser demon cowering like a dog with its tail between its legs and at other times a bloody brawl followed. Jagged teeth tearing at demonic flesh and muscular, demonic limbs pounding. Vicious engagements of teeth thrashing, jaws biting and fists striking with wicked speed.

The result was never good for the loser and sometimes not even for the winner.

And despite the unruly behaviour below, shame continued to express itself across Michael's angelic good looks. In the space of a few seconds, Michael's face tilted upwardly, taking with it a frown for company. Michael took his eyes off his demonic enemies as he looked to Madame Liz.

She sensed it more than ever; he yearned for comfort and understanding.

"I cannot help but feel that I am in some way and in part to blame. Had I carried my duties out diligently, then these demonic terrors would not be the rulers of my home."

Gabriel immediately shot his head around. "You are being too hard on yourself," replied Gabriel. "I have been your friend and fellow archangel since the dawn of time."

Gabriel pointed to the grounds below. "Heaven's defeat is not the result of one archangel's doing."

Madame Liz did not want to dwell in the past, for her existence was largely spent looking into the future.

"I have seen it," she blurted. "Since the heavens had been taken over, tensions amongst angels and spirits alike have been running high. You needn't have psychic foresight to see this. But we have not suffered alone." Liz shifted her focus to the infighting and quarrelling directly below; two winged demons in the middle of a gruelling fight.

"They fight for domination. This is what you get without good leadership.

"Lucifer has taken his trusted General to Earth and together they spread havoc and wrong doings. I have no doubt we will have a trail of disaster to clean up after he has finished with his reign of terror, but we cannot do it from up here."

A slight change in the subject matter.

"Lucifer!" Madame Liz spoke his name with a vengeful tongue. "His egotistical desire to seek revenge on Earth has left his troops without leadership and direction. They don't know what they are doing, they taunt us and then they fight within themselves. When they have had enough they taunt us some more and then they fight amongst themselves some more. Their behaviours are predictable and pathetic."

Liz looked up at her archangelic friends.

"I have seen it. Heaven shall have its day and we will once again be the rulers of heaven's sacred grounds. The time to fight back is drawing nearer."

Michael and Gabriel looked down and caught the gaze of a single winged demon standing solitary in his own little patch of heaven.

The demon could not miss the opportunity to tease the two archangels and gifted psychic.

In a cheeky sort of fashion, the demon fell backwards into the billowy white floor. The clouds of white would normally flow gently and lovingly and wrap itself around any of heaven's occupants.

But this was a demon from the depths of hell. The floors of heaven with its natural, soft billowy movements were replaced with quick, sharp and erratic shifts. The white puffy clouds jerked left and right and up and down, but despite its agitated type movement, it still sought to wrap itself around the demon like a quilt blanket.

After all, heaven's misty ground cover was designed to offer unconditional comfort, warmth and love, but it always reacted differently to creatures originating from the depths of Hades.

The demonic soldier specifically checked to see that he had the attention of the two archangels.

They were looking.

The devilish creature played it up.

Like a dog scratching his flee ridden back, the demon rolled and twisted around in the white cloudy puffs, occasionally stopping to ensure the eyes of the archangels were still upon him. He playfully licked his lips and rolled his eyes as if there were no greater pleasure. He taunted the angelic duo in a way to say this is all mine and you can't have any of it.

After a handful of minutes, the demon got bored with his antics. He stood up and then looked directly at Michael. He dusted himself off with the dignity of royalty, taking smooth, steady, methodical strokes. He played on this for only a small while before returning his cheeky smile upwardly.

Just when Michael thought he had seen the end of this little demonic charade, the demon's mood changed suddenly.

The demonic soldier turned his head and revealed his snarling teeth, showing them off to the grounds below. The growl only lasted a few seconds, but the demon blatantly displayed his disgust for all that was heavenly.

He then twisted his head around, as fast and as far as it would go. He let his head swivel, an aggressive twist from left to right. The head movement not complete without a demonic spit on heaven's floor. The demon then proceeded to rub his green sputum mess into the ground with his right foot, like he was stepping out a lit cigarette.

Finally, the evil one walked off, never giving the spiritual trio above any further eye contact. His fun and games were over, but not before the archangels' faces stiffened with anger. If looks could kill, then this sinister creature would be cut up into a thousand pieces.

Unfortunately, a stalemate existed. The hellish-bound creature was amongst friends below and the angels had retreated to the upper levels of heaven.

This was the way of life in the spiritual world and for now, there was nothing more that could be done.

Liz left Michael and Gabriel to sort out their affairs, but she left knowing her vision to be true. The attack to remove the invading demonic terrors once and for all would happen, and soon. It was inevitable, for she had watched this unfold before her psychic eyes, knowing the intimate details of events yet to happen.

The heavens would return to their rightful owners and as everyone around may have anticipated, the victory would not come easy.

From the emotional stress to the physical casualties, the cost of any war is far too expensive.

Calling All Souls-Part II

Up until now, the archangels had worked hard preparing everyone, organising and practicing. Everything was in place ready for the execution, but the declaration of an all-out attack was always put off for another day.

And in recent times, Madame Liz had spoken wisely; there was no use putting off the inevitable; the crucial moment to strike and take back their sacred land had arrived.

In the upper layers of heaven, Archangels Michael and Gabriel worked frantically to ready their troops. Unlike countless times before, this was not a practice drill.

Down below on heaven's main grounds, the demons took their positions. None the wiser to the preparations above, they gathered for another one of their psychological warfare outbursts.

All together the evil ones mustered, their purpose to collectively shout to those above, with the primary objective of undermining heaven's ways and manipulating the psyche of all that stood in God's light. All this for the sole driven purpose of destroying heavenly morale.

This was the art of spiritual and psychological warfare.

The demons gathered in a tightly packed circle. They came from the extreme corners of heaven's land, walking towards a central band of winged demons, walking towards the organisers of this up and coming heavenly taunt.

The winged twelve stood centrally watching their circle of soldiers grow outwardly. Too many to count, a sea of dark skinned bodies gathered, stretching out to the distance, the wrangle could be heard throughout.

They gathered, at the ready to follow the orders of the winged leaders but for a selected few, small clusters of fights broke out across heaven's land. In some areas, serious infighting, in other parts, they pushed and shoved, all in the name of displaying superiority.

The leadership amongst the evil ones was breaking down again, the unruliness of the crowds far worse than it had ever been previously.

One of the winged leaders, frustrated with all the commotion, flapped his large leathery wings to gain a better perspective. A nearby brawl between two foot soldiers, the rowdy crowd egging on the punch-up.

The winged demon had seen enough and was quick to swoop in as he barged between the brawling duos, throwing both fighters apart.

They hit the ground hard, but were quick to pick themselves up. The winged leader let them be as he set out to fly high above the gathering crowds.

The leader grew angrier by the second. He shrieked it out with bitter high notes, deafening and for all to hear, the order to stop their petty bickering followed. His command not just for the ears of the two nearby fighters, but for all the scuffles that were breaking out across the land.

His demand a threatening promise in his language of shrieks and screams.

"The next to disobey will be dealt with by the twelve of us."

The speech hit its mark.

Across the land, demonic scuffles were being pulled apart by onlookers. Demons all around were breaking up the fights of their comrades and then, just in case they had missed it, they communicated the threat of their winged leaders.

In a short space of time, fighting activity had settled and not too long after, demon far and wide resumed with their activity of gathering without further incident, converging as they were instructed to do, forming a circle whose circumference was larger than large. This was the way it should have been in the first place, with hundreds of thousands upon hundreds of thousands coming together for a common demonic cause.

There the demons all stood, shoulder to shoulder, winged demon next to foot soldier, restless, agitated, but at the very least, focussed on the up and coming task at hand.

Hidden in the upper layers of heaven, just as many in number looking down at the masses below, but today they would look back with a distinct difference, for today they were ready to declare their war.

The devilish gathering was at the ready, anxious to begin their psychological, demoralising, raging screams at all that was heavenly. To disgrace angel and spirit above, to ostentatiously flaunt in a manner that heaven's land was now ravaged by hellish beast.

All this and much more would be put forth in today's gathering, for this was the art of demonic psychological warfare.

At the ready, all waited for the demonic command to start.

Winged demon and foot soldier looked upwardly towards their heavenly counterparts. All waited for the signal to go, the centric most demons would lead the way.

Suddenly, the twelve flapped their wings, rising and spreading out. They hovered above their comrades in arms.

It would be on their signal, and in unison, they cried out their command to begin.

It quickly followed.

Hell-bound voices booming into heaven's atmosphere. The roar pulsed through the heavenly layers with amplitude and sinister vibration.

They snarled, screeched and yelled at their angelic enemies above. The demonic language howled across the different levels of heaven for all to hear.

In previous times the angels and souls would have angered and shouted back their reply, but on this occasion, all of heaven's best rained down on the unsuspecting masses below.

In next to no time, angels and sprits attacked from all angles.

Their numbers evenly matched. Together, warmongering angel and combatant demon interlocked. Millions sprawled across heaven's billowy floor, a fight to win back their rightful land.

In a soul-destroying counter attack, the war was on, the outer rim of the circle thick into battle, the inner circle of demons struggling desperately to get outwardly to join the fight.

The angels and spirits came down fast, grabbed, kicked and struck with ferocity. Hellish beings gave just as much back.

The battle now took to the air for those who had the ability to fly. Thousands of winged demonic bodies and angelic beings rose up from the fighting crowds and jockeyed in mid-air.

They faced off with one another whilst the ground troops remained engaged in deadly arm to arm combat.

The hovering angels looked at winged demons and vice-versa. The moment was short lived, the angels charged and without hesitation, the demons struck back. A clash of bodies, grappling, twisting, striking as battle raged above in mid-air and on the grounds below.

The casualties began, the sounds of the cracking of souls popping everywhere like Chinese fireworks.

His first victim, the cry of victory rang from Archangel Michael's mouth.

A fallen and beaten winged demon left lying to the floor beneath him. Michael hovered in mid-air and watched as two spiritual, heavenly fighters pounced on the unconscious body of the winged one. They both struck with several punches until the cracking of the soul was heard soon after, the demonic body vanished forever, the hellish soul now seeking its rehabilitation in accordance to heaven's law.

The angels had that part covered as well.

For those who passed on in battle, the spiritual guides and counsellors were there to help spirit and demon alike, to assist with the process of rehabilitation. Very quickly all counsellors were busy with their supportive duties, dealing with dead souls from both sides.

The fatalities soon re-appeared everywhere, many lying in the foetal position, worse for wear, as it was always meant to be. Shocked and traumatised in the after-life by their deaths, unable to comprehend neither their deaths nor their re-appearance onto heaven's sacred land.

Thankfully, all counsellors were at the ready to help. That is, all bar one.

For in the archangelic plans to rage war on demons below, the rehabilitative process had been given due consideration and consequently planned for.

But there was one thing the archangels couldn't change for today, Pam's rehabilitative skills and counselling expertise would be notably missed.

Chapter Twenty-nine
The Heart of Madness

This was a land of sorrows, a place of eternal damnation. It went by several other names as well, but was best known as hell. Either way, the smell of sulphur and brimstone lingered and was ever-present.

Together, in the darkness, Pam and Johnny stayed.

~ * ~

It was me, Pam.

I had to make a bold decision and pick my bearing. I couldn't be one hundred percent certain I'd be walking in the right direction, but the gut wrenching urge to go that way and get up and over the hilly face was too hard to refuse. Wasn't sure what I would see from there, but I felt if I followed my instincts and climbed up high, then I'd at least be able to get a different perspective on this place.

That was only a short time ago. Now, Johnny and I were way above the valley floor. This was new terrain, a way out. I could only hope and pray that from here, we could both find our way back to heaven.

But for the moment, I turn my attention to Johnny.

There is nowhere large enough to lie down and Johnny has no choice but to sit. His shoulders are arched forward and his head is slumped downward, that is until he tilts his head up at me.

I catch his weary eyes. They look at me as if he hadn't slept in a week.—If we weren't in the afterlife I would say he looked like death warmed up.

I felt bad. I knew what was required of the situation, but I simply did not have the luxury of giving Johnny the time he needed to rest and heal.

I had only one thing on my mind: The quicker we got out of this place, the better, but in the process of climbing that steep hill face, I fear I may have pushed Johnny too much, too soon.

What is done is done. I cannot turn back the clock and besides, I feel better having left Hell Central and the valley floor below and if Johnny could think with clarity, I know he would feel the same.

But I see it in him. The torment and torture of having his soul violated by Sebastian and Lucifer. He is suffering and so for now, I will do his thinking for him. I will be his protector and aid until such time that he can stand on his own two feet.

I look at him. His head is in his hands. He no longer looks to the outside world.

"Give it time, Johnny. All will be okay with time. You'll see!"

Johnny is resting up against a large rock now. I will give him his rest whilst I work out my next move.

This isn't going to be easy. I don't have the viewpoint I thought I would have. My vision is largely blocked by densely packed, sandy toned boulders. The land before me is too cluttered with rocky formations for me to see too far into the distance.

And yet, how strange. There is a tinge of light in this land which allows me to distinguish between the colour of rock and of the surrounding land. This is an evil ridden land whose thick, shadowy blanket of dark grey is like a gloomy night time sky.

I am confused. What to do?

It's a long shot, but I turn to the young man seated nearby.

"Which way, Johnny?" Maybe he can help, but probably not. He looked back at me with eyes filled with despair.

Having worked with my fair share of traumatised souls, I dare not begin to imagine what he must be going through. I sympathise for his anguish, but I don't give in.

"C'mon, Johnny, you must remember. You have been here before." I try so desperately to get him focussed on something other than his own inner torment. If only he can recall his previous experiences with the after-life, then

this will serve to help accelerate the process of healing.

Remembering is always a good first step to recovering, but I can see that Johnny is not quite there yet.

I try a different tact and fill in the blanks for him.

"You cast God's light in this valley. Back at a time long gone, you completed the task the angels asked of you. When your angelic-sent mission was completed you were sent back to Earth with no memory of your time in heaven. Back then, the angels wiped your memory clean, but I know they only took it from your conscious mind. Your subconscious never forgets. The events of your journey through hell with Tony by your side are recorded forever, there to access when the time calls for it. C'mon, Johnny, concentrate. Reach down deep to the farthest recesses of your mind and access those events. Your history and knowledge of your past experiences within hell will help heal. PLEASE, JOHNNY, PLEASE TRY! Your knowledge of this place will help us get home."

I said it to him, I pleaded with him, I SHOUTED it to him, but it was no use, his eyes were distant and his manner, non-responsive.

As a trusted counsellor to all that walks heaven's sacred land I know this to be true. Johnny needs his space to recover and with time, he gradually will.

Unfortunately, time is not a luxury we both have.

If I can't get a response then I will go it alone. I will gather my own intelligence on this land before we go off together again, so best I do what I set out to do in the first place and look for a better vantage point.

I am ready to go it alone until I hear my name called out.

The voice is faint and gravelly like a bad case of laryngitis, but on the plus side, at least Johnny is alert.

Surprised, I turn. "What is it, Johnny?" I asked.

His arm quivers as it hangs in mid-air. Before it flops back down by his side, if only for a second or two, he points me in that direction.

I acknowledge the help. "I'll be back in a moment," I said.

I set off in the direction as Johnny directed me and quick step in and around the boulders. Their formation tightly packed, but I get around them or even climb over them. The farther I get from the hill face, the more sparse the boulders. The land before me begins to open up.

I look around the rocky landscape, whose boulders are a free mix and variety of sizes. Some are no bigger than a basketball while others stand taller than me and broader than an automotive vehicle. A good range of all sorts of shapes and sizes.

But size doesn't matter for I am soon walking in and around the rocky obstacles; there is no need to climb over them anymore.

A few minutes of walking and weaving in and out and then I see it.

The land ahead opens up to be relatively barren. Up ahead, far fewer rocks, more open ground. It's dark and I struggle to see into the distant horizon, but at least the immediate grounds before me areobstacle free.

I think of Johnny. Even with my help, he will struggle with the first bit, struggle where the rocks are tightly packed. Getting up and around the dense landscape will be a challenge for both of us.

But I am a little excited, it's not all bad. If I can get Johnny into the open land, then navigating this barren, hellish landscape from there on won't be so difficult.

The first part of our journey together will no doubt be the most trying, but I have never known Johnny to back down from a challenge. We can do this. I will go back and tell Johnny the good news.

~ * ~

It's me, Johnny.

I am sitting up against this rock, nursing my head. The pain is terrible, a migraine of the splitting kind. The thudding in my mind punches the inside of my skull, my upper vertebrate rattle with each pulsating thump.

I re-adjust my sitting and rub my forehead; it seems to help a little.

This rock has my back and the ground is surprisingly comfortable. It's hard to refuse the temptation and so I drift to sleep.

In what seems like next to no time, my blissful rest is disturbed. I hear her voice.

"Johnny wake up, Johnny wake up."

I look up and it's Pam. Before I know it, she has returned. She gives me a second or two to come around and leans over. The next thing I know I am helped to my feet.

Reluctantly, I stand, with muscles as sturdy as jelly.

I continue to battle with my inner demons. I feel like I am in a deep water well, all alone with darkness all around, paddling frantically, trying to stay afloat and with no bottom to touch.

I am tired and worn out. How does one escape from themselves? This is not like me. I would gladly trade this body for another if I could, but I cannot. I struggle to muster up all of my strength, but all I can manage is to work with what I have, which is so little.

But I try.

Wherever possible, I will conserve my strength and maintain my integrity. Do I have a choice?

Then I hear her sweet gentle voice again. It's soothing and re-assuring at a time where my thoughts and energy reserves are in total chaos.

I am not sure what I would have done if Pam wasn't here with me.

"Give it time. It will all go away eventually." I hear her say her words of comfort.

"Lean on me some more." Pam takes her first few steps and I follow as best I could.

Suddenly I am hit with irrational thoughts. I can't help but focus my attention on my mixed up emotions.

I feel no connection to my inner self. I feel as if my skin has been peeled back and I am exposed to all.

The ragged rawness burns within me, this in-the-moment exhilaration that exists within my mental processing is quickly followed up by confusion and black despair.

The disabling sorrow.

All these emotions smashing at me. I watch it come towards me, all at once, crashing into my mind's eye like a driver watching mud slung across his entire car windscreen.

I struggle to comprehend what's in front of me. It takes too much my energy, both mental and physical. I am way too exhausted.

I have no clear sense of time passing, no framework, nothing. I see the darkness all around, but I yearn for God's light to heal my injuries.

I am walking with Pam if that's what you call it. My legs are moving, but mostly they drag along the hellish landscape. My weight is supported on Pam's shoulders as my legs struggle with moving functionality.

I grieve.

"Not another step. I need to rest," I say as I let go and collapse to the hellish landscape.

I am well enough to at least notice the look of disappointment stretched across Pam's face. We both know it. I have only taken a few steps. I can't go on.

Here, at least I can lie down and so I do so. I feel most comfortable curled up in the foetal position. I shut my eyes to get away from it all.

I don't want to look at the dark greys of hell any more. I want the world around me to shut down for a while.

I will come back when I am good and ready to do so.

I never spoke these words to Pam, but I hope she understands.

Time passes ...

I am woken up again, but this time I feel rested.

"Sorry, Johnny, I fell asleep as well. I guess we both needed our rest time. Feels like the best shut-eye I have ever had," I hear Pam say.

Funny enough, I felt that way, too. Felt like I'd slept for days and days, but it couldn't be; or could it?

I take a good look at the environment before me, absorbing the depressing detail of rocky boulders, barren land and dark, gloomy grey colours. The familiarity of it all hits me suddenly like the pain from a slap in the face. I know this place, I know where I am and I realise where we need to get to.

I need to stand; my instincts tell me to try.

Sluggishly, I rise on my own now, looking a bit like a puppet on a string. I don't need Pam's help anymore, although I do catch her look of amazement.

I steadily rise to eventually stand. It feels like I completed the world's best magic trick and for my efforts, I give a gentle bow and in return get a little happy clap of applause from Pam.

I still need her assistance, but I won't be leaning on her as much.

My thinking a little muddled still, but I now know what I need to do, where I need to go and I yearn for my return to heaven's homeland.

The landscape ahead is free of creature or demon and I know the journey to be long.

I have been here before. I travelled here with my friend, Tony. We did as the angels asked of us. I know this place. I know this land.

Hell had forever been burnt deep into my psyche, once forgotten, but now has surfaced like a blue whale.

My attention turns to my legs. I know I am far from a full recovery, but I have the strength to carry me onward.

I look to Pam with the biggest smile on my face.

"Head for the light in the distance, Pam. The small sparkling light which shines no larger than a bright star in the night time sky. This is our heavenly beacon pointing the way."

I pause for a brief moment to look at the landscape behind me. I frown at this place and all that it stands for. I return my gaze to the journey ahead. Instantly, a wave of happiness shoots through my soul. With the prospect of hope and faith, I cannot resist the temptation to put a smile back on my face.

I have never been so certain of anything as I am now. I speak to Pam with a confidence I long missed.

"Yes this is it. This shining light that glows for us in the distance, this is God's light. It is telling us to come home."

Chapter Thirty
To the Outside World

Johnny's spiritual soul was somewhere on the outskirts of Hell Central. His physical body, however, walked the Earth. And to the people of the world below, Johnny still appeared as he always had—as a man of the cloth.

To date, no one had suspected a thing. The demon Sebastian had successfully stepped into Johnny's body; his primary interest was to remain incognito and to use Johnny's body as a vehicle in which to move about and complete his unearthly mission.

Using Johnny's body, Sebastian would have his revenge on Tony.

Dressed in his black and white priest attire, Sebastian stepped outside the rear church doors to meet with the Thursday early morning chill. A plume of misty vapour formed with every exhale only to dissipate soon after.

Up above and stretched across the entire sky, a singular cloud, spread out as if it had been done with a butter knife. Its wafer thin consistency interfered with, but did not completely block out the picturesque blue.

Despite the unhindered sunlight, the rays came with no warmth; Sebastian's exhaling cloudy bloom a testament to that.

Outside they stood, side by side. Next to Sebastian and in spiritual form, was his master, the devil.

Sebastian stood in his human form, rubbing himself down, trying to generate some frictional heat.

Lucifer stood next to him, a ghostly apparition unaffected by physical, earthly concepts like temperature.

"A little cold, are we?" Lucifer laughed out his sarcastic question.

A quiet snarl was Sebastian's reply.

"Well then, down to business," Lucifer remarked.

"You shall wait here. Keep yourself hidden inside this church. The other will come. It's only a matter of time. And then you know what needs to be done."

Sebastian, shut his eyes and bowed his head in acknowledgement. The lines between servant and master clearly drawn.

"This couldn't have gone better for us," added Lucifer in his language of clicks and shrieks and screams. The pitch used was varied; high and low tones.

"We have one of their souls," said the devil.

"And I will take care of the other," Sebastian snarled.

The trusted General had pleased his master. The grin on his red devilish face went from ear to ear.

In a rush, the devil blurted out, "I will go. I have the need to walk in physical form. I shall seek her out so I may occupy her body."

Sebastian understood.

Soon after, Lucifer's spirit vanished as he left for Alison and Allie's home. The devil would soon possess and use Allie's young form as a host, much like Sebastian used Johnny's. There was, however, one distinct difference.

Lucifer had Allie's permission to possess. Unfortunately, the same could not be said for Sebastian and his host body, Johnny.

Sebastian turned and walked back into the warmth of the church.

It had been a little over an hour since Lucifer left. With every passing minute, the air chilled down even further. Winds had picked up, blowing harder and longer than they had before. The one giant singular cloud above pressed against the sky like a quilted bed sheet, its stretched out formation had grown fatter, its dark grey billowy base threatening the Earth below with pending rainfall.

Still, that would not stop him from his mid-morning cup of coffee with his friend.

Tony knocked on the rear church door.

"Jesus!" Tony exclaimed, startled by the sudden door opening before he had a chance to finish his third tap.

Tony was waved in, his friend, Johnny (Sebastian), was silent.

"What's wrong with you—cat got your tongue?" Tony asked with a friendly cheekiness in his tone.

Sebastian (Johnny) would not give away his identity just yet and ignored the question. Instead Sebastian led the way as he walked directly into the church office, expecting Tony to follow.

Tony shut the rear door and kept his position.

"What's up?" he shouted across the room.

Sebastian popped his head from out of the office entrance, waved in his friend and then returned to the confines of the room. At this point, Tony could no longer see his friend.

"Okay, if you want to play silly games then I'll play along." Tony followed Johnny in. By the time he entered, Johnny was standing on the other side of his desk.

Upon his entrance, Johnny looked back at Tony, a cheeky grin emerged. Johnny tilted his head down a little so as to raise his eyeballs at him.

"Enough is enough, Johnny. What are you up to?" said a frustrated Tony, but the only response Tony could get out of his friend was a slow lifting of a solitary finger to be placed over his lips, indicating silence.

Then Johnny lowered his hand and tapped at the upper most drawer of the church office desk. He looked down at the drawer and tapped it once. He then looked back at Tony in the same way he had before, head tilted down, eyeballs raised.

He repeated the action for a second time, stretching the moment out. Sebastian appeared to like taunting the young human.

Tony's frustration deepened. "This isn't funny anymore." He demanded a response.

But instead, Johnny resumed eye contact with Tony, and then in a slow and steady pace, methodically raised a solitary finger to indicate silence.

On his third attempt, instead of knocking at the top drawer, Sebastian opened it with a furious, jerky action. When the table drawer came to its full extension, the drawer locked into its position, the contents rattled inside with some spilt over to the floor. Amongst the items to fall out of the top drawer was the sunglasses box. As both of them watched its path, it travelled in a parabolic trajectory, hitting the floor nearby.

Tony instantly recognised the pair as the one Johnny had given him which gave him the strange visions on the waterfront.

Johnny moved closer to them and bent down and placed his hand on the case. From where the sunglass case lay, he flung it and its contents at Tony. Tony reacted instinctively and juggled the catch for a second or two before successfully retaining the hold.

Johnny made the notion to put the glasses on.

"Are you in your right mind?" asked Tony. "We spoke about the strange visions. This is no ordinary pair of glasses!"

There was a reply with two notions of movement.

The first was the standard solitary finger of silence. The second was the action of opening up an imaginary case and lifting an invisible pair of sunglasses onto his head.

Johnny's motive was quite clear. He was, without a solitary word spoken, unmistakably displaying what he wanted Tony to do.

Tony stood there in disbelief whilst an uncomfortable silence lingered in the air if only for a few seconds.

Johnny, now standing back on one side of the preacher's desk with Tony on the other.

Sebastian was bent over slightly, his arms stretched out on the table as if he were supporting his body like a tripod supports a camera. The classical head down, eyeballs up was the look of the day.

Tony looked at the sunglasses and then looked up at Johnny. Tony rubbed at his forehead, confused by the distant reaction of his friend and of the request of the moment, but he succumbed to the notion to raise the glasses to his head.

Uncomfortable yet willing, his eyes fixed on the floor, a large gulp of nervousness in his throat. Ever so slowly, Tony put the dark shades to his eyes. Before fixing them to his head, a momentary pause, the decision was made, this would be done with eyes closed and so they went on, his eyelids shut tighter than a bank vault.

It was hard for Tony; he didn't want to open his eyelids. In the dark he remained where it was safe. He would have liked to have stayed that way forever, but the sound of a sudden WHACK changed everything.

In his frustration, Sebastian slammed the office desk with both his hands, not hard, but loud enough. The sudden sound breaking the silence, the message distinctively clear.

Tony reacted as expected. In a split second after the thud, Tony flashed open his eyes, although he didn't look up, his gaze remained on the floor as he waited. He feared the worst.

What visions would these glasses bestow on him now?

Tony waited for the floor to light up in flames of reds and yellow, much like the water had done so on that day back when he went fishing. He waited a second and two and three and four.

The clock ticked on and yet there was nothing.

Finally, a young Tony felt relieved. With his adrenaline-filled heart settled from the non-event, it was time to look his friend in the eye to now address his unruly behaviour.

Tony looked up. His mouth open and ready for speech and yet in a split second, it was like someone had cut out his vocal box.

Startled by the vision before him, Tony staggered back, unable to speak a word. Shocked in horror, what he saw was not the face of his friend, but the face of the beast, Sebastian.

His snarly face, shark-like teeth, black beady eyes and skin as black as black was disturbing.

An electrifying shiver rushed through his body. Goosebumps raised along both forearms followed very quickly after.

Tony took a few more steps back. With more space between him and Sebastian, it was time for a double check. He removed his glasses only to see the face of his old friend.

Something wasn't right. This didn't make any sense at all.

He placed his shades back on his head and there was no mistaking the change. The face seen through hell influenced lenses was clearly demonic.

But this time, there were two more entities, ghostly in appearance and floating above and to the rear of Sebastian.

For the moment, Tony was distracted by the presence of his mum and dad. They looked worried and had every right to be.

Frantically, Charlie and Mary blurted out their words.

"Run for your life. This is not Johnny, but a beast from hell," shouted his mother.

"Johnny is here in heaven with us. Protect yourself, this thing before you is out to get you," shouted his father.

Sebastian turned his head at the invading ghosts; they were not welcomed.

He turned over to the right and screamed at Mary's spirit. She vanished almost immediately.

As Sebastian turned around to the left, Charlie got his last words in.

"Remember the dream. The changing face. Run for your life and get as far from this creature from hell as you can," Charlie shouted out in desperation.

Charlie finished what he had to say and then copped an ear bashing from Sebastian. A second later, his spiritual form also disappeared.

Sebastian watched on to make sure his ghostly intruders did not re-appear. He continued to snarl at the invisibility to ensure his unwelcome guests were gone. Through the evil pair of lenses, Tony watched on as well as listened.

In that moment, Tony remembered, his mind's eye instantly homing in on the dream.

~ * ~

Suddenly, Lucifer's face interchanged with Johnny's. One moment Johnny's face was superimposed on the devil's, the next vice versa.

Johnny's face smiled at me, but when the change occurred—when the devil's face placed itself back on Johnny's head, it looked back at me with a thriving threat.

The superimposing went back and forth, back and forth with Johnny's time becoming shorter and short lived until all I could see was the look of the devil.

~ * ~

It was incomprehensible and yet how could Tony deny everything before him. The changing faces of the demon as witnessed through a pair of unholy sunglasses were as he had dreamt only a few nights before.

His heart should have been pounding, his chest heaving with eyes wide open, but instead, the only thing racing around was his thought processes. With a calm body and a not so calm mind, Tony frantically searched his strategic thinking for options and potential opportunities.

His ghostly parents now gone, leaving nothing behind except two single trails of vapour, one to the rear and above Sebastian's right shoulder and the other to the rear and above his left.

Sebastian snarled and cursed at the space behind him; his head swinging left and then around to the right, never settled on which direction to bark his cursed shrieks to.

The leftover ghostly mist hung in the air like the smoke of a cigarette, burning away in an ashtray. Its wavy, foggy trail lingered for a bit longer and then disappeared altogether.

A little more shrieking to the empty air and Sebastian was convinced his unwelcomed intruders were well and truly gone.

Sebastian then turned his attention to Tony.

Tony removed his glasses and held them in his right hand.

Tony had to ask the question, for he knew Johnny would not have gone down without a fight. Tony pushed aside the horror of it all as his face changed to one of disbelieving.

"My God, Johnny—what have those bastards done with you?"

Tony wasn't expecting a response. The silence lingered in the air as human and demon faced off with one another.

The silence was short lived.

As Sebastian had done for Charlie and Mary, he did so for Tony. A final and clear message for this young man.

Sebastian let out his threatening scream. A curdling yodel, mainly in high pitches, of clicks and shrieks. Its evil harmony shook Tony's soul to its core.

His collected calm moved on, Tony couldn't stop his body from trembling.

Sebastian stood upright, the beast on one side and Tony still on the other side of the table. By this time, Tony was positioned more near the door; if he had to make a quick exit then he was at the ready.

Sebastian raised his human arms and Tony's eyes followed. Tony's head tilted upwardly, watching, as Sebastian's fists were raised high and clenched tight.

Sebastian's (Johnny's) priestly attire was flexed to the max. Sebastian raised his arms a little higher, the stitching in the underarm falling apart from the strain, the sound of material ripping was visibly evident.

Like a starter's pistol, the sound of the material ripping was the prompt for Sebastian's next move.

Tony watched for it.

His fists came crashing down, the sound of the impact like clapping thunder. There was no holding back. His arms came down hard and fast, fists clenched tight with rage. The thump was sharp and loud, leaving slightly cup-sized, caved in indentations into the desk top.

Sebastian then made his next move, stepping out slowly and methodically towards Tony. He casually strode out from behind the table and walked towards him. Tony kept his distance at all times, putting as much space between he and the beast without losing sight of the enemy.

It was time to exit the office area, but there was one thing left to do before he did. The thing before him was not his friend. He no longer required the sunglasses to see through to the truth.

He threw the pair violently at his former friend.

Sebastian moved his head a little to the right, dodging the projectile. They hit the wall behind and fell to the ground. There they remained.

Sebastian and Tony maintained their distance, Tony now standing a little to the outside of the office doorway.

In a flash, Tony made a promise to himself, one he would die keeping, if that's what was called for.

Whoever or whatever had taken Johnny, had picked on the wrong guy and the thing that stood before him was going to be brought to justice, one way or another.

Tony backed his way into the main part of the church, keeping a constant space between him and the creature in front of him. At all times, he was considering his options and planning his next moves.

Up until now, their eyes had been fixed on one another.

Very quickly, the pain for the loss of his friend quickly turned into downright anger. Nothing would stop his resolve—ever.

Convinced he would need them, Tony looked around, quickly assessing the items of the chapel. What he saw helped him to formulate his plan.

Tony had to make a fast decision.

There was plenty around to choose from. Many of the items could easily be transformed into a defensive weapon if it were in the right hands. Tony, being an accomplished martial artist, made his choice.

He grabbed two solid brass candelabras, ripping the candles away from their resting places. Their broad base and solid, lengthy shaft made for an ideal weapon.

They were like two fighting sticks in his hands, each close to two feet in length. Tony held onto the solid stems, using the broader base as the part that he would strike with.

He swung them around, quickly becoming accustomed to the movement and motion of his new found weaponry. Tony swung and struck as if he were striking an invisible opponent. He only had a minute or two to perfect his defensive and attacking skills. The fight would soon be on.

Sebastian and Tony were near the church altar now, standing a few metres apart. Tony lured the beast into this patch of the church. It was about as big an area that Tony could find to strike and attack, uninterrupted by obstacles, trip hazards and the like.

Tony took his fighting stance, Sebastian snarled back his response.

Tony's left foot forward, his left hand holding out his first candelabra five or so inches from his chest. The weapon was angled out, pointed to this beast in priestly clothing. This would be his lead weapon, intended for blocking or to be used as a feint should the opportunity present itself to strike first. His right hand, withdrawn and level with his right ear, the base of the second candelabra pointing upward, ready for the powerful counter swing.

Tony was at the ready. It was a face off, standing only a few metres apart, a young Tony faced off with an old demon.

Suddenly Sebastian and Tony were not alone. Tony could not see them, but as Sebastian's place of origin was spiritual, he retained the ability to see into the afterlife.

Sebastian was distracted as he looked to his left and to his right, he looked beyond Tony, looking above and beyond his left shoulder and then to his right.

Tony quickly looked around, the impression Sebastian gave was that there was someone standing behind him, but Tony saw nothing.

Quickly, Tony returned his gaze to the front, but Sebastian continued to be distracted, looking everywhere; his eyes shifting to the left, then to the right and then all around.

Lead by his dead parents, Mary and Charlie, Tony stood between them without realizing they were even there. Behind them and in force, seventy seven spiritual counsellors appeared.

Sebastian saw everyone, Tony could see nothing.

They all spoke, some individually and then all at once.

"You will not take my son!" shouted Mary and Charlie at the demon beast.

"This is a place of worship, you have no place here. Be gone, you demon," shouted a counsellor from the rear left.

The remainder of the group of spiritual advisors to the immediate left and right of Sebastian put forth their holy threat. Seventy seven voices in unity, including Tony's dead parents; the sound deafening and distracting to Sebastian's ears.

There they all stood in their ghostly presence.

"Listen, you who hate the good and love the evil. We have gathered here, your reign of terror is done.

"For the day of the Lord is near, and as destruction from the Almighty, it comes.

"We are here to deliver the message, as we speak, the battle in heaven rages and we are the victors.

"Your time has come; this is a place of worship, a place of holiness.

"RETURN NOW - TO YOUR PLACE OF DARKNESS."

Then they repeated it over and over again.

"RETURN NOW—TO YOUR PLACE OF DARKNESS."

"RETURN NOW—TO YOUR PLACE OF DARKNESS."

Suddenly, Charlie appeared for his son. He gave him this one message. "We are here in spirit and will not leave your side."

The vision of Charlie was gone as quickly as it had appeared.

Johnny growled back a reply, more directed to those spirits surrounding him rather than to Tony. Sebastian wanted them silenced as he shouted back in his native devilish screams and clicks, but they wouldn't stop.

They chanted their message repeating it over and over and over.

"RETURN NOW—TO YOUR PLACE OF DARKNESS"

"RETURN NOW—TO YOUR PLACE OF DARKNESS"

Whilst Sebastian was busy dealing with a room full of unwelcomed spirits, in the distraction, Tony went on the all-out attack.

A barrage of swings hit the beast. Solid brass candelabras hit with incredible accuracy and remarkable strength.

Tony attacked the spots on the human body for maximum damage. Face, throat, groin, solar plexus, temple and jaw.

In between swinging candelabras were low kicks to the knees and upper thighs.

One after another, the vital points of the body took a pounding.

Sebastian covered up, but the barrage of strikes combined with the deafening spiritual messages overwhelmed the beast.

After several hits, Sebastian crumbled to the ground; a powerful right kick to the upper thigh saw to that. Sebastian on one knee and bent over took to more beatings, this time over the back of the head and shoulders.

The devilish reply was definitely unearthly. Sebastian's tone changed. He no longer threatened Tony in his shrieks and growls, but instead begged for leniency.

There was no mercy here, no consideration given to his plea. Tony did not stop. He struck Johnny's body to the ground; a final left handed swing of the candelabra came from nowhere. Up, around and to the inside, the swing large and exaggerated, as Sebastian crouched on all fours, looking like a dog about to drink out of his bowl, Tony's candelabra swung around and up to hit the side of Johnny's right temple.

Battered and bruised, Sebastian was down for the count. Laid out like a knocked out boxer, in and out of consciousness, this was as far as the counter attack went.

Tony dropped his candelabras and ran for the rear door. He exited the rear of the church, leaving the door slightly ajar. Tony moved like the wind. He couldn't get home fast enough.

Sebastian struggled to keep his eyelids opened and very quickly fell into unconsciousness.

Within the hour, Tony was home.

Tony's mind was racing with one thought after another. One hour of driving had not answered all his questions, but quite the opposite; he had become quite agitated and very anxious.

He parked his car, ran to and unlocked his front door. His nervous hands made inserting the key a little harder than it normally would be, but a jiggle here and there and the key found its place. Once inside, Tony checked around the home to ensure that everything was locked, closed and secure.

The job was done. He could now breathe a little easier. Off to the lounge room sofa, Tony fell back into his couch with a giant sigh of disbelief.

The nervous energy kicked in, his heart pounded with the thumping of a jackhammer. He could still feel the throbbing strain on his forearms from the candelabra swings. His body had been running on adrenaline and still was to a degree, although it had calmed a little. This, however, did little to stop the muscle aches and strains from surfacing.

In his after panic, the reality of it all had to be faced, although it was still unbelievably true.

His friend was dead.

The thought hit him with a ferocity far worse than the beating he'd just given Sebastian.

In the solitary confines and safety of his home, Tony put his finger to the base of his eyes and wiped away the first of what would be many a tear.

Chapter Thirty-one
Angela, Allie and the Devil

Lucifer and Allie stood face to face. She sensed he was nearby, but could not see his spirit. Either way, the young girl knew what to do.

"Stand here, sweetheart. Out in the open and not near any obstacles. We wouldn't want you to hurt yourself," Angela said as she moved her daughter a little farther from the kitchen dining table.

"Are you ready for him?" asked Angela and Allie nodded back eagerly.

With an excited smile sprayed across her young, angelic face, the young Allie then closed her eyes in preparation for her possession.

He didn't hesitate.

Lucifer stepped in like walking into a room. She could feel him; it hit her like a rush of cold wind. She felt it all the way from her face and head to the tips of her toes. A tingling, sharp, icy sensation.

It was so refreshing.

Inside Allie, two souls were working in harmony for the common (evil) cause. Allie's persona would have to take a 'step back,' allowing Lucifer's to dominate. She allowed this to happen willingly, but still, this process took a few minutes to work out.

A few more seconds here and there and then her eyes shot open; Lucifer's spirit was in control.

Angela recognised the difference immediately. "My Lord!" Angela cried out. She then curtsied as a sign of her respect. Lucifer ignored the response and turned to gaze outside the kitchen window.

Angela could see it in her daughter's face. Irrespective of the souls within, the expressions and emotions still remained the same as they always had. Her mother could read her daughter like a book.

Angela watched Allie, or more accurately, watched the devil gaze into the distant sky. He was clearly agitated and as much as a mother would want to run to comfort her daughter, Angela resisted the urge to do so.

Angela kept her silence for a little longer and waited. She gave him the time he needed to come to terms with whatever was on his mind. A moment later, Lucifer turned, and Angela instantly saw the frustration. It had set like concrete across Allie's beautiful little face.

It was not fitting that a young child should have to endure such stress and anguish, but Angela had to keep reminding herself. Allie was not in control anymore. The look and emotions belonged to Lucifer and at times like these, it was hard to comprehend, but Angela had to take a deep breath, calm her thinking and very quickly accustom herself to the fact that this was now her demonic master.

The differentiation came even quicker when her daughter spoke. This was not her sweet voice, but a deep resonating, directed and one-way conversation.

He spoke like an arrogant General speaks to his troops.

"Those fools - how can I reign on Earth when I have imbeciles governing heaven," Lucifer spoke out loud.

"I am not sure I understand, my Lord."

"Heaven!" the devil stated. "All this work and for nothing. All of heaven was ours. I loathed the godly light and its crisp blue sky. The fluffy clouds sweeping at your feet, the serene pleasantries all around were sickening to my stomach. But to watch the angels suffer. The torment on their souls. To control and to have the power for all that heaven represents and say that it was all mine and no longer part of God's land anymore. The look on their angelic faces. How I teased them and at the same time, as they stared down at me angrily, I looked back up and watched their suffering. Now, that was all worth it."

Lucifer paused for a moment. He calmed his voice, but it still boomed with the sound of a cannon.

"We sacrificed it all. Heaven was all mine and soon I would reign on Earth as well," he spoke.

"But I had to leave idiots in charge," he said, smashing his fists on the kitchen bench.

"We are losing the battle up there. In the near future, the angels will regain control of their beloved land. They will drive my soldiers back to where they came from and so with angels in charge, my time here is threatened."

Lucifer turned and grabbed Angela on both shoulders. Her young and short female body reached upward and gripped her mother's shoulders with gentle strength. Lucifer succeeded in grabbing Angela's uninterrupted attention.

"My time here may be limited. We must act swiftly," Lucifer blurted.

Angela hurried her words. "Yes, my Lord. Anything. Anything at all. I am here to serve."

Lucifer was about to speak again when he was distracted. A message coming through of the spiritual kind. He paused for a few seconds, a look of concern washed over (his) her young face.

With Angela still in his grip, he added, "Take me to the church. I must get to his church quickly."

Angela knew exactly where to go and instantly went for her handbag and car keys.

~ * ~

Deep in the spiritual world, on the barren wastelands of hell, Pam and Johnny were slowly making their way towards the Transitional Border, a place where dark meets light, where one step can mean the difference of standing in hell or being in heaven.

A small sign, like a bright star, shone for them, a beacon to bring them home. It was way ahead in the distance.

Side by side they walked.

Pam looked over. Slowing her pace down a little, she let Johnny take the lead. She wanted to watch and observe and see how Johnny carried himself.

Johnny continued to walk with an asymmetrical gait, favouring his left side still. It wasn't as pronounced as it had first been, but it was clearly noticeable.

It was certainly understandable and Pam should know, after all, she was a counsellor to the souls and was very familiar with what one goes through when one has taken on a beast from hell.

Lethargy, weakness and confusion were all part of the journey of rehabilitation and time was the only thing that would eventually make it all better, but despite Pam's observations and her knowledge of traumatised souls, Pam had to ask the question.

"How are you feeling? Better?"

"I wish you'd stop asking me that. You only asked a few minutes ago. Things haven't changed that much since the last time you questioned me," Johnny light heartedly replied.

Pam smiled.

His quirky sense of tone with a hint of sarcastic humour was how she remembered it to be. All and all, a good sign Johnny was slowly returning to his former self.

"I am tired, though," stated Johnny.

Pam looked around and pointed up ahead. It was only a small distance away.

Soon after they camped in the middle of five rocks, which circled around them giving them more than enough space to get comfortable. The rocks were wide and tall enough to (mostly) hide their seated bodies away from any would be prying eyes.

Johnny was quick to put his back up against one of the boulders. He soon dozed off, his healing body needing some much needed rest.

Pam was comfortable in her assessment of the immediate area. The rocks should keep them from any nasty and unexpected surprises. They were about as hidden as they could be on this godforsaken land.

Glad enough to get to their new found haven of rest and comfortable enough with their security, Pam laid herself on the barren surface. She curled up and shut her eyes.

They rested for several hours, although neither one of them ever really knew how much time had actually passed. They needed their sleep and plenty of sleep they did get.

Many, many hours later, Johnny was first to open his eyes. He stretched out his arms and casually looked around. Pam was lying nearby and as for everything else, nothing had changed. It was the same old dark, dreary and depressing scenery without a single soul in sight.

But still, Johnny moved cautiously, keeping his body in line and below the surrounding boulders.

Johnny sought out his beacon of light, popping his head around one of the boulders. They were the only two in this barrenness, but still, Johnny stood cautiously.

Looking ahead at his light of hope, looking out to the beacon that would guide his way home. Johnny found it, smiled at it and then sighed a heavy sigh.

It felt as though it was a hundred miles to the Transitional Border and not a soul nor any provisions between the two places. And in the spiritual world, a provision was not food and water, but rather God's healing light. A source of godly energy that fed the souls of angels and spirits, more nutritional and far more beneficial than any food source or exercise regime on Earth. Not only that, but the comfort and love of fellow angels and spirits were also a provision that was dearly missed.

Johnny looked around.

A few seconds was all that was needed, for there was certainly no great inducement to stay in this territory and every incentive to get up and move onwards.

Johnny leant over Pam's body. She looked so relaxed and he hated to do it, but he knew they couldn't stay.

"Pam, get up! Get up! It's time to go." His gentle voice woke her.

A stretch and a moment to get on her feet and they were soon ready to go.

"Doesn't look any closer, does it?"

There was that quirky sense of humour again. Pam couldn't help but giggle back a reply to Johnny's sarcastic question.

And so off they went.

~ * ~

Back on Earth, outside the church, Angela and Allie (Lucifer) rushed into the rear of the church door. The door burst open from its position of how it was last left by Tony; slightly ajar.

"Sebastian," shouted Lucifer in a demanding voice, but there was no reply.

"Sebastian, he shouted again as both he and Angela walked towards the main church area.

She spotted his lying body first. "Over there," stated Angela.

Sebastian in the form of Johnny was about to sit upright. Still dazed, he rubbed at his head, trying to ease the throbbing pain.

Angela looked the priest over. The gashes and bruises, his bloodied face was not a pretty sight.

"There has to be a first aid box here somewhere. I'll go find it," said Angela. She rushed off.

"What happened?" asked Lucifer, his face and voice riddled with anger.

Sebastian kept rubbing at his forehead; he may have been a spirit of hell, but in his human host form, he felt every last bit of his battering, and for the moment, the pain demanded more attention than his master.

Angela returned with a first aid carry case. A small box, but filled with the necessary items. Gauzes, tissues, disinfectants, iodine patches were all laid out so she could get to work, but instead, Sebastian brushed this aside and stood.

Groggy like a beaten boxer, but able to stand firm, for whatever reason, Sebastian wanted the warmth of the sunlight and walked outside to get some fresh air.

Lucifer and Angela let him be.

Sebastian got outside and alone he stood.

He looked up at the day. The glare caught him by surprise. Sebastian, although tempted, did not rub at his eyes for the fear of ripping his eyelids out. Sebastian knew his time to be limited, for Johnny's body would not keep without its soul intact. With every passing hour, every passing day, the skin would lose its moisture and become stiff and flaky and although not visible to the naked eye, well inside the body, the rich, red, soft muscle would become infested with multiple spots of death and decay.

This was the downside of completely vacating a body of its soul and stepping in.

Already, parts of the flesh and many of Johnny's internal cells had died; the rotting brown patches spreading and growing across the intracellular fibre, the rusty colour of death, spreading inside his body like a vicious cancer.

Perhaps he had a week, maybe a little bit more or maybe a little bit less, but ultimately, the bacterial armies of Johnny's body were growing out of control. They had begun their attack, the decay of their work already eating away at his insides. The bruises and cuts to his body did not, nor would they ever heal, for the body he now possessed was a walking, soulless corpse functioning, not in repair mode, but rather, in decay mode.

Ultimately, Johnny's body was a human being which walked and talked, but one which remained soulless.

Sebastian had enough of the sun, the glare was overwhelming. He went back in to meet with Lucifer and Angela.

Angela was waiting at the rear kitchen table with her first aid accessories. Allie (Lucifer) was nearby.

Angela waved Sebastian over, patting down the kitchen seat implying for Sebastian to take a seat.

Lucifer intercepted Johnny. "Don't bother. This body is too damaged. You will not be able to keep your identity safe."

"We could try covering up his wounds with makeup. Make them blend in with skin tones. The rest can be covered with clothing," stated Angela.

"You needn't bother," replied Lucifer.

Allie spoke to Sebastian in his native language of shrieks and clicks and screams. A varied pitch of yodels and nonverbal communique.

Soon after, Johnny's body slumped to the floor. It lay there motionless.

Angela looked up concerned. "What did you do to him?" she asked frantically.

Allie's pretty face looked up to the sky. What Angela heard was a unison of voices.

Her young child's sweeter than honey tone and the unmistaken deep resonating sound of Lucifer. There was this strange, but distinguishable harmony, a synchronicity of two completely opposed sounds.

In unison they spoke. "My army will need leadership whether in battle or retreat. We have sent him back to be the General he is. For me to stay on Earth, Sebastian will need to succeed in heaven."

Chapter Thirty-two
Defeated

Archangel Michael had given up on keeping count.

He hovered high in the air watching his last dark demon fall to heaven's floor. An archangelic right hand strike to his jaw saw to that.

The demon fell with the speed of a soaring hawk and hit the ground hard. His unconscious body was not dead yet and a nearby heavenly spiritual soldier would soon change that, turning to pound on the unconscious demon. He hit him a further three times until the unholiest of cracks was heard.

Another demon off to heavenly rehabilitation, thought Michael.

The archangel turned to find his next victim, but instead, his next victim had found him.

With only a split second to react, Michael spun a full turn with his wings outstretched to their fullest. His enlarged, swan-like white feathers held firm, slapping the flying demon off course.

Soon Michael and his would be demonic attacker were interlocked, spinning and tumbling, grappling and striking.

This one fought hard and gave as much as Michael gave back. But the warrior class angel was stronger and resilient. Exchanging blow for blow, there could only be one winner.

And soon this demon was falling to heaven's billowy floor as fast as the previous one. The demon's fate to be completed by spirited ground attack.

Michael had to shake this one off. The strikes to his head dazed him a little.

He had to get away from this space and so he flew higher and higher, gathering speed and putting distance between he and the aerial fights below.

He was now much higher in the heavenly stratosphere. Any impending danger was way beneath him. For the first time in a very long while, Michael could gaze down on the aerial and ground attacks.

Angel dodged at charging demon. Demon struck at oncoming angel. On the grounds below, swarms of spirits and demons brawled.

There were numerous gang-like attacks with the understanding that killed casualties were preferred over injured ones. In other words, the only good demon was a dead one.

Sprawled across heaven's land, battles enraged, Lucifer's army spread out wide and far, gradually being pushed back towards the Transitional Border.

Michael could see it. Beneath him, and all around, it was as clear to him as the white billowy floor below.

Inch by inch, heaven was gaining ground and with things going the way they were, soon heaven would be free of their raiding demonic terrors. Soon, heaven would return to its rightful owners.

Suddenly Michael noticed a strange shimmer in the not so distant horizon. He watched him phase into heaven and the moment he recognised the face of Sebastian, Michael wasted no time in making a beeline to him.

Within a second or two of phasing in, Sebastian knew the command that needed to go forth. Focussed on the fighting below, immediately and in his native language he demanded, "Hold your ground."

The demon General never looked above his shoulder, for if he had, then he would have seen the approaching archangel. Michael, on the other hand, never took his sights off his unsuspecting target.

The archangel thrust his wings, raised them high and thrust them down again.

After a few more flaps, the time had come to pull his wings back. Michael had gathered the speed he desired and impact would occur soon.

Sebastian barely had the time to throw out a second command. The momentum of angel and demon coming together had them spinning in circles until it all came to a stop, Michael's forearm securely locked around the demon's throat.

Sebastian wriggled like an eel and made indescribable efforts to slip out of the clutches of the archangel.

Michael would break the General's spiritual neck before he'd release his stronghold.

Using Sebastian as ransom was the key to stopping this terrible war.

Across the lands below and in the skies above, the fighting gradually came to a halt. Bit by little bit, all other angels and demons separated to look up at Michael restraining Sebastian.

Michael and Sebastian hovered high enough for all to see.

A nearby winged demon threatened to intervene. Charging like a bull, the dark angel heroically flew at Michael, but Michael shouted out his angelic scream, a siren of trumpets, deafening to all around.

Michael tightened his chokehold grip further, forcing Sebastian's head to tilt back.

Sebastian shot out his hand, the universal gesture for stop.

His flat palm faced outwardly towards the charging demon and the demon was quick to pull up and retreat from the immediate area.

The uncomfortable pain was sprawled across Sebastian's face for those near enough to see.

For those too far to tell, the chatter amongst the devilish troops below soon spread to inform all who were unaware; the time had come to leave God's land.

With anger raging in his soul, Michael could rip the demonic General's head clean off, if he had to. Sebastian would not be given voice nor breath for pleas of clemency.

Enough was enough; the archangel threatened the demonic crowds around.

"It ends here and now."

Michael slowly spun with Sebastian restrained, a three hundred and sixty degree viewing. Michael ensured he got the attention of all.

"One last chance. We will fight to the end and from this point onward; the first casualty will be your General."

Sebastian wriggled some more, but his attempt to escape was futile.

"I will ensure that in death, your General stays in heaven for an eternity. I will place him where no demon will ever see his ugly face again. I will spend my days torturing him. Your loss will be my pleasure."

It was a stand-off, perhaps even a bit of bluff attempt by the archangel. Would he or could he do all that he had stated?

Either way, both sides were at a stalemate and this was used as the tipping point, to highlight to the demonic army that they had their fun, they did their bit, heaven paid the price and suffered for it, but now... It was time to go home.

There was confusion amongst the demonic ranks below. Hellish conversation rose from the crowds, demon talking amongst demon.

Sebastian tried to speak, or more to the point, tried to throw out his commands, but Michael did not allow Sebastian to voice. Michael knew his enemy and he very well understood the ways of the demonic General. He suspected Sebastian would not favour a retreat and given half a chance, would command his troops to stay and fight, to the bitter end if they had to.

Thankfully the troops below had grown tired. It was not hard to see morale had drained from them long ago.

One by one they turned, and then ten by ten, hundred by hundred, thousands by thousands.

They turned to walk home.

Angel and spirit stood their ground, watching their invading terrors retreat to where they belonged. The dark was their home and they were not welcome where God's light shines bright.

Michael held onto Sebastian. He would neither speak nor be released until all had crossed over from the Transitional Border.

They stood and watched for the longest time, the first demon only metres away from crossing over to the dark.

The angel and spirits couldn't wait for it and cheered to the heavenly skies. A cry of joy rang out for all to hear, and although the demons had not fully retreated, the angels celebrated for their victory. Angel and spirit embraced and cheered.

~ * ~

On the other side of the Transitional Border, Pam and Johnny were making their way up the rocky incline. This last little bit of ground would take them home.

"I remember," Johnny stated with excitement. "I remember being here," he said again. "I was running with Tony, we were trying to get away from the demons who were chasing us and I tripped. I slipped on these damn pebbly rocks below. I lost my footing big time and Tony and me... We went down for a good crashing."

Johnny then smiled as he turned to Pam. "We are nearly there. We are nearly home."

Just then, Johnny noticed them coming.

The first of many a demon crossed back over. The demons had not seen them, not yet anyway, but Johnny definitely saw them.

A second or two later Johnny saw more of them come across the Transitional Border; too many to count, too massive in numbers.

By now, the retreating army had crossed over by the thousands, walking in rows that ran the length of a major city.

Johnny caught the eye of nearby demonic foot soldiers. There was nowhere to hide and far too many to fight.

A decision was quickly made. A promise to himself that he would die keeping, if this was what was called for.

Johnny stepped forward and stood in front of Pam. If only in a protective sort of way, he put himself between advancing demons and Pam.

Up ahead, there was still a bit of space between Johnny and the retreating demonic army.

Johnny felt her touch on his shoulder.

Pam looked at Johnny with proud eyes and then proceeded to hug him as if she were hugging her grandson. She held him in safe grandmotherly arms as she whispered into his ear.

"Close your eyes, we won't feel a thing. Our deaths will be quick and we can die knowing heaven has been victorious. Our heavenly brothers and sisters will see to our rehabilitation."

Pam didn't even wait for an answer, but tightened her protective arms around Johnny.

Johnny closed his eyes as was asked of him. Pam did the same.

Pam said her final words. "Do not fight the demons. Do not resist their attack. It is best we keep our eyes shut and let our deaths be swift."

Johnny knew Pam could sense his nod of recognition. He trembled with the fear of his impending death. Pam held onto him tighter. The more protective Pam became of Johnny, the less he trembled.

Johnny waited for it.

He didn't have to wait too long.

It had begun, the first of thousands of demons to walk by them.

Johnny winced at every passing growl, hiss and demonic curse. He could feel Pam do the same.

They waited with eyes shut, fearing the worst. Which demon would be entrusted with their demise? There they stood in each other's arms, being cursed and bumped into.

The screams rocked his soul. Johnny trembled nervously waiting for the inevitable.

"Keep them shut, Johnny," whispered Pam, re-enforcing the message she had put forth earlier.

Johnny kept his eyes closed and by now could sense demons were all around. The sound of the chatter and squeals and shrieks grew louder with the merging demonic troops, as did the clatter and crunching of millions of marching feet.

Nearby demons passed by the spiritual pair as they continued to shriek their evil curses at them. They bumped their leathery bodies into their clean heavenly spirits as they walked by.

Johnny waited for it and waited for it. The bumping and screams continued, but nothing more.

Pam lifted her head from his shoulder and looked around. Johnny soon opened his eyes and did the same. They separated, but stood close to one another.

The demonic army, by this time, was all around them, marching back to their home.

The snarls and bumps and curses hadn't stopped, but for the very first time they could see.

They needn't understand the demonic language to sense the message that was coming across.

The demons wanted them out.

The time had come to finish with the fighting and simply return to home.

Pam and Johnny hesitantly pushed forward. They got the cold stares and the growls and evil barks, but no demonic soldier lifted an arm or threatened to strike.

Johnny kept his gaze down, coward-like. Pam did similarly as to not provoke or upset.

As demons passed by in one direction, Pam and Johnny gently shuffled forward in the other. They pushed and weaved their way ever so gently. They took the demonic bumps and the hellish abuses, but dare not engage eye to eye contact.

With gazes fixed on the hellish landscape, they slowly made their way towards the Transitional Border.

It seemed like an eternity had passed, but they eventually both got through it.

Pam and Johnny stopped and looked and observed.

They waited and waited and waited, looking back at the sea of demonic bodies slowly making their way farther and farther into the depths of hell.

There was some distance between them now.

Pam and Johnny would have jumped for elated joy. They would have screamed it out aloud, yelled that they survived their trip in hell, but in fear of risking demon retaliation, they simply celebrated their collective well-being quietly and cautiously.

The time came to ignore what was behind and pay attention to what lay ahead.

They were there, the Transitional Border, where separation between heaven and hell was only one step away.

Johnny turned to Pam.

"This is it, Pam. We are home."

Johnny stepped aside and did the gentlemanly thing. With a wave of his hand and chivalry entrenched in his blessed soul, he gestured for Pam to be the first to cross over.

Chapter Thirty-three
Funeral for a Friend

Tony gently wiped away at his eyes; the salty, dry trails of tears still tingling on his cheeks and lower face.

He looked towards the priest who was about to speak.

"We gather here today to celebrate the life of Father John Black, who has now returned to his home with Our God, The Father."

With grieving sadness, Tony sat in the front row of the church, on the aisle corner of the pew, his grandfather to his immediate right and Johnny's parents, brothers and sisters seated next to Arthur.

His Uncles Jack and Chris sat in the row immediately behind Tony and as for the rest of the church, it was jam packed with friends, family, fellow priests and the church regulars.

The crowds crammed the inside of the church and then flowed out into the front courtyard. Speakers and screens had been set up for those outside. They all came to pay their last respects to Johnny.

And although no-one else suspected a thing, there were also some unwelcome guests amongst the gathering today. Angela and Allie (Lucifer) were seated in a pew around the midsection.

A priest from a nearby church performed the service. He was a little older than Johnny and had mixed with his company on several occasions.

He spoke from the heart; speaking about a loss of colleague and friend, the loss of a spiritual leader, one who was so young and yet so dedicated to his congregation and community.

In next to no time, the priest was about half way into his service when he spoke these words. "Let us pray for his soul in the afterlife."

That statement hit hard.

Tony flashed back to his encounter with Johnny and Sebastian. Johnny's soul had left for the afterlife long before his body died. What Tony battled with back then was not his friend, but a demon in disguise. Tony wanted so desperately to address the congregation and share his truth with them, but Tony was sensible enough to know it would be unwise to do so and besides, who would believe him? Sebastian possessing Johnny's human form would have to be his secret for now.

Tony turned his attention back to the priest and his speech about God and the heavens. Tony's emotions swelled inside him.

The priest continued and a little while later, was nearing the end of his service. For Tony who was so caught up in all his worries and sorrows, minutes seemed to fly by like seconds.

The priest made another remark about Johnny's life. "Here was a man of the Earth and a rock to his community," the man of the cloth said. He paused for a brief moment and allowed his words to sink in.

With his eyes closed tight and for the shortest of times, Tony truly believed that this could only be one big bad dream, but alas, the silence was quickly replaced with the calming melodies of the church choir. As soon as the church organ played its next few bars, Tony was once again left with the harsh reality that his friend was dead.

The music played and the choir sung their hymn in perfect harmony. The priest took some time out and sat in his seat next to his podium.

Before the Father was seated, Tony dropped his head into his hands, sobbing uncontrollably.

In a flash, Tony felt Arthur's comforting arm around his shoulder and it didn't take long before Tony leant his head into his grandfather's protective bosom.

In times like these, in times gone by with the passing of his grandmother and the death of his parents, his grandfather was always nearby.

Tony took his attention away from the front podium to gaze across to the tan stained coffin with its lid shut tight. It was overflowing with colourful wreaths and bouquets of mixed bright coloured flowers.

Johnny would have liked the floral arrangements. In such sad times this was a pleasant reflection for Tony.

A small round table positioned nearby with a framed photo of Johnny in his priestly attire smiling to the camera.

Tony focussed in on the photo, almost hypnotised by Johnny's wide brim smile and full of life eyes.

The next thing he knew, Tony was watching the priest approach the table. The choir stopped and the priest now had Tony's undivided attention.

"Funny!" the priest remarked. "This single photo, in so many ways, captures everything I knew about Father John Black."

The priest placed the photo back down on the table, carefully positioning it as if it had never been lifted.

With teary eyes, Tony watched the Father walk back to his podium and take his position behind the microphone.

"His graduating photo; I remember the moment well," the Father said with light-heartedness in his voice.

Addressing the crowds, the father spoke crisply into the microphone.

"I never knew Father John in his childhood and had only come to know him through his journey into becoming a priest. We had become friends during this time and for me and many others I can only say this." The priest paused, his silence replaced with subtle crying whimpers coming from those who had gathered.

"I could not imagine this man being destined for anything other than the profession he chose to follow. This was his calling; I have no doubt of this. His passion and dedication to living the life of a priest was more inspiring to me than any other I have come to see."

With a short pause, Tony and the Father's eyes met. The Father knew Tony and knew their friendship history. In this small moment in time, the Father shot across his caring smile.

The Father then returned his gaze, looking across to the framed photo.

"I saw it in the man they called Father John, pardon me… Father Johnny Black."

The priest now addressed the mourners in and outside the church.

"Always compassionate, caring, willing to lend an ear, sympathetic and full of life, but never taking life too seriously. These were the qualities of the man whose life we celebrate today."

Tony felt the gentle squeeze on his shoulder from one of the uncles from behind and turned to see his uncle, Jack, retreat his hand. Tony appreciated the gesture.

The service continued and soon the time had come to finish with the closing rites.

The father glanced across to the front aisle, briefly making eye contact with those closest to Johnny. He looked across at Tony and Arthur and then moved his gaze across to Johnny's parents and siblings. He gave them all a brief look into his sympathetic eyes. At this point he finished his sermon with his final praise.

"You will be dearly missed, Father Black. To all who have gathered here today, let us go in peace to live out the word of God."

~ * ~

The sermon had finished a little while back.

There were streams of people shuffling their way out of the church. All of them were here to pay their last respects to Father Black.

All who were here were worshippers of Christ and all he represented, all except for a mother and daughter who worshipped a darker, more evil entity.

Angela and Allie waited in the corner of the front church courtyard. Angela watched as the crowds slowly made their way out.

Angela waited patiently, waiting for the one.

Deeply seated inside her soul and sharing in the possession of Allie, Lucifer spoke.

"There he is."

Angela watched as Tony walked out, his arm around Johnny's grieving mother, Marlene, offering her comfort in her time of need.

Soon after, they eventually settled in separate parts of the church courtyard doing the social thing, talking to familiar faces and being there for one another.

A short time later, Angela watched Tony break off from the crowd. He appeared to want to isolate himself from everyone else.

Tony had walked away from immediate family, but not before he got a comforting pat on the back from his grandfather. All could understand and appreciate that Tony wanted the time to himself.

Just then, the hearse made its way around. It was a traditional black Cadillac. It pulled up near the front of the church and everyone paid one last respect, bowing their heads as Johnny's coffin was carried out by six representatives of the church. Clergymen and priests from neighbouring churches had the honour of doing so.

They approached the Cadillac, rear door swung high, the rear of the car lined with a fine velvet type carpet, its shiny blue colour almost fluorescent.

They juggled the wooden box onto the edge of the rear compartment and then slid it to the front. Rollers on the hearse's rear helped glide the coffin into place.

One of the clergymen then placed some of the floral arrangements as neatly as he could on top and around the tan casket, setting them on the blue velvety carpet and placing a few of the floral wreaths on top of the wooded lid.

Before too long, the Cadillac's back hatch was being shut gently as to not crush the delicate stems, buds and colourful petals.

It had been made clear at the start of the service. The burial was a private matter and only by invite.

Angela was not planning on going, even though she knew Tony would.

Angela continued to watch over Tony. In his isolation, he seemed to stare at the hearse with sad eyes. His cold emotion made her heart warm with joy.

As the car pulled away, Angela caught Tony's attention.

Their eyes locked.

"Go to him," Angela heard Lucifer (Allie) say.

"Yes, my Lord."

Angela walked towards Tony, which had him gaze back with curiosity.

Angela approached the part of the courtyard where Tony had chosen to isolate himself from the rest of the family. He may have wanted this space to himself, but in next to no time Angela would be joining him.

Angela didn't bother with the niceties of introductions; instead she went straight to the point of her visit. "I would like you to have these," Angela said, handing over the demonic pair of black sunglasses.

Judging by the look on Tony's face, a mixture of shock and disbelief, he knew exactly what was being handed to him.

With a slight hesitation, Tony reached out for the sunglasses.

In a playful type of tone Angela spoke. "Go on, put them on."

Tony couldn't.

How Angela loved taunting the young man.

"Come now. Are you afraid the boogie man is going to get you?" Angela snuffed a laugh and then stepped back a little so Tony could get a clear view of little Allie (Lucifer), who was standing only a small distance away.

Allie knew her part in this. She bobbed up and down, excited-like. She bent and extended her knees slightly and waved her arms as if she were trying to get the attention of someone.

And that she did. Across the church courtyard Tony noticed.

For the last time, Angela stated her intent, only this time, she thrust her command out at Tony, speaking down to him in a manner more fitting of two men about to go fisticuffs in a bar room brawl.

"Put the god damn glasses on." she insisted with a harsh and direct tone.

Her angry face was a glowing red, her eyes penetrating. The look must have hit its mark because in his vulnerable moment of sorrow, Tony only hesitated for a second or two before lifting the shades to his eyes.

"Now that's a good boy," she said with a calmer, sarcastic tone.

Tony put them on and looked back at Angela.

"Oh," Angela stated in the same sarcastic tone of hers. "These aren't for me, sweetheart." Angela then guided her hand towards Allie.

They stood several metres apart, with a clear path of sight. Allie was at one end and Tony at the other. Angela stood near Tony, but made sure his vision of Allie was unobscured.

Tony looked across the courtyard at the young Allie bobbing up and down. As soon as he looked at her, he saw him, the unholiest of the unholy, bobbing up and down with his red leathery skin, short tapered horns and killer white eyes. Through the demonic pair of shades, the devil's features appeared as though they were transposed on Allie.

The instant Tony looked over, he shook his head with major disbelief as if someone had slapped him out of the blue.

Angela knew Allie's true form had been revealed. Angela stood nearby while Tony tried to make sense of the unthinkable.

The vision was as Tony had experienced with Sebastian taking over the body of Johnny. Similarly, with his special pair of glasses, Tony could now see through to the true form of Allie.

Angela didn't stick around for Tony's feedback. She turned to walk away before he had the chance to question her. And for her first few steps, Angela walked away, leaving behind her sinister laugh to linger.

Chapter Thirty-four
Home Heaven

Mary stood by her husband and gazed her eyes over the landscape.

The white billowy clouds rolled gently over heaven's surface with a likeness and texture of cotton wool balls moving cohesively, gently being tossed around, as if they were being blown about by a gentle wind. Mary then ran her eyes to the sky, admiring its simple and yet most beautiful shade of blue.

Mary was lost in the tranquillity of it all. The sheer beauty before her, in the nicest way, stabbed at her to the very core.

They both stared at heaven's sky for the longest of times, virtually hypnotised be the ever-present calm until eventually, Mary broke her silence.

"It's not until you lose it that you truly appreciate what you had."

"It's good to have heaven back," added Charlie.

Behind Mary were spirits and angels rejoicing over their recent win. The demons had retreated a little time ago and so it was, across heaven's sacred grounds, victorious celebrations continued.

Mary fixed her sights back to the horizon where in the far distance, two silhouettes suddenly appeared. They were distant shadows, their faces couldn't be made out, but Mary knew, as did Charlie.

With nervousness in her voice, Mary spoke to her husband. "They've got to be okay?"

Mary went for them, but Charlie held her back. "Give them their time. Let them bathe in heaven's light, just for a little while longer. Let them have their time to acclimatise."

With an impatient restlessness, Mary held back.

Pam and Johnny's silhouettes grew as they steadily walked closer and closer. Time seemed to tick by ever so slowly for Mary, but after a little while, Pam and Johnny's faces came out of their grey shadows.

Mary couldn't wait.

Seeing the face of her mother was like letting off a starter's pistol at a runner's sprinting event.

Mary took off and ran as fast as her legs could take her and soon after, had her arms around Pam and Johnny in one giant embrace.

"We're alright, darling," stated Pam. "Johnny's been through a tough time, but nothing that heaven's light and a bit of rest won't fix," Pam added.

Mary broke off her embrace and lovingly looked at the two of them.

"It's good to see you both. We were so worried," Mary said.

"It's good to see you, too," replied Johnny.

The re-acquaintances were only beginning to take off when out of the blue appeared the Virgin Mother and Archangel Michael.

Mary hadn't noticed them beforehand and Pam, Charlie and Johnny appeared as surprised by their sudden appearance as well.

Archangel Michael wasted no time in separating Johnny from his group of friends. They soon stood, the two of them, a small distance from the rest of the gathering.

The warrior class angel was in private conversation with the former clergyman. Mary looked on, puzzled by the secrecy of it all. Mary then cast her eyes across to the Virgin Mother, who stood alone. The Virgin Mother was focussed in on the archangel. It was as if nothing else in the world mattered.

There they all were with their focus of attention on what appeared to be a rather intense conversation between Michael and Johnny.

From where Mary stood, she could not hear a single word. Whatever was being said to Johnny, it was for his ears only.

Johnny took everything in, hanging onto every archangelic word. The nods of acknowledgement flowed back and forth, as did the conversation.

And towards the end of this strange encounter, Michael spoke as if he were a General directing his next plan of attack.

Johnny listened. There were hand movements, gestures and detailed conversation from Michael. Johnny didn't speak much; in fact he didn't say a word.

Mary watched the duo in the distance. Archangel Michael was thorough and Johnny had this look of determination on his face, as if he were being asked to undertake the holiest of tasks. And one thing was for certain; whatever was being said, he had Johnny's full cooperation.

"What do you think that's about?" whispered Mary to her mother.

"I haven't got the foggiest," was Pam's reply.

The archangel finished his discussion and gave the former clergyman a gentle squeeze on the shoulder as would a friend to his buddy.

Johnny turned his head to face Pam, Charlie and Mary. Mary and Johnny's eyes locked for the briefest of moments and then, as if every passing second were critical, the archangel wrapped his giant swan-like wings around Johnny. He squeezed him like a boa constrictor to his next meal. It didn't take long. Johnny collapsed as if his heart suddenly stopped beating.

The Virgin Mother didn't hesitate. She walked up to Johnny's lifeless body and kneeled beside him. "May God's love be with you always," she said and then kissed Johnny on the forehead. By the time she stood, Johnny's spiritual form had vanished.

The events before Mary were too overwhelming to process. Johnny was her son's best friend. Johnny was like a second son to her. Mary's protective, motherly instincts instantly kicked in. Mary frantically ran up to the Virgin Mother.

"What have you done with him?" Mary questioned, clearly distressed by what had happened.

The Virgin Mother brushed her gentle hand on Mary's face and turned to walk away. The Virgin Mother had a way of transmitting her love and peace. The injection of heavenly calmness shot through Mary's soul as quickly as flashing lightning.

The Virgin Mother walked away, leaving Michael to explain.

Mary's burst of instant calmness dissipated shortly after and she was back to her worried self. She turned to the archangel and asked the same question of him.

"What have you done with Johnny? Has he not suffered enough? Let him be," Mary demanded.

"He is in need of rest and heaven's light. Can you not see that?"

requested Pam of the archangel.

Charlie was about to add his concern to the conversation, but the archangel interjected.

"The devil walks amongst the living. A wolf in sheep's clothing. He possesses a willing host. A young girl who will willingly give her life to follow in Lucifer's footsteps. The girl's mother is also as dedicated to hell's ways as her daughter. They are working together with Lucifer so he may eventually fulfil his evil plans for the people of Earth."

"Yes, I remember," said Charlie. "Mary and I were in that house. I followed the young girl into a room, but this was no ordinary room. This was a place dedicated to the worship of the devil. Worship of evil."

"The devil possesses her soul as easily as one puts on his clothes. And when possessed, the young girl's soul lives in harmony with the spirit of Lucifer. He is then free to use her body as a vehicle to do as he wishes," said the archangel.

"And what does all this have to do with Johnny?" asked Charlie.

"The next time the devil decides to possess his young female host, well, let's just say that the little girl's soul will shortly be on its way to heaven and Johnny's spirit will take its place. His spirit will be waiting to have a few words with Lucifer."

~ * ~

Down on the Earth below in the middle of the night, young Allie lay asleep in her bedroom.

Her eyes suddenly shot open and quickly after, her chest heaved as if she had surfaced from a deep ocean dive, trying to suck up as much oxygen as possible. Her breathing steadied and soon a smile spread across her sweet young face. Her spirit was well and truly gone, an express trip, soon to be counselled by heaven's best way up above.

Johnny was now the driver of the young girl's body and with no doubt in his mind, he would follow the archangel's instructions to the letter. Yet all along, Johnny couldn't help but add his own little agenda to this situation.

Johnny lay in Allie's bed, his (her) eyes wide open and the cheekiest of grins planted across her little face. And in light of the fact that at some time in the near future, Lucifer would look to step into his little girl's host body and the inevitable encounter of good vs evil would then take place.

There was no issue here. Johnny looked forward to meeting up with Lucifer once again. And yet, Johnny couldn't help ignore the vision in his brain, this personal agenda of his.

In the still of the night, Johnny (little Allie) lay wide awake, the smile painted across Allie's / Johnny's face ripped out its warning in advance to Lucifer.

The first time I met with your evil spirits I was unprepared, but now I will wait patiently, and eagerly look forward to our next encounter, thought Johnny, *For the next time we meet it will be you, Lucifer, who is unprepared.*

Chapter Thirty-five
Meeting in a Park

This place was somewhere Tony had visited many a time before and more often than not, his friend Johnny had accompanied him. It was a nearby suburban parkland, a place Tony loved going to. At times it was to catch up and have a friendly relaxing chat with a close and personal friend and at other times, this place presented the opportunity to get out for some fresh air when the occasion called for it; the parkland was a perfect location to simply chill out from the day to day hustle and bustle.

That was back then, but times had changed. Johnny's physical form had now been laid to rest, never to walk the Earth again. And as hard as it was for him, Tony would have to accept that he would have to move on with life without Johnny by his side.

Tony sat alone at a parkland bench. Here was a place that held a lot of history for the two friends. The pleasurable memories of having Johnny for company on practically every visit he ever took to the parkland proved to be so hurtful today.

Death may be the ultimate finale, but how does one push aside a friendship that was so close; closer than the best of brothers. Call it what you will, but for Tony, this setting was more than just trees, greenery and play equipment.

Deep down, Tony's soul ached with a sorrow so strong, it felt like his insides were being eaten up, leaving nothing but a big black nauseating emptiness.

The memories of a former mateship continued to rush into Tony's conscious mind. It pounded and tore at the very core of his soul.

Tony looked out to the open green grass and trees for a bit of comfort. At times like these, nature's serenity had its way of doing a little bit of revitalising of the soul, but one does not get over the loss of a lifelong friendship that easy.

Overcome with sadness, Tony felt them coming; armies of teardrops at the ready. His eyes watered a little more than usual, but he stopped it there. Tony was determined there would be no tears shed today. Not here, not at this special place.

Tony got himself together and a moment later distracted his thoughts by pulling out a folded envelope from his top pocket; for today, there was another reason for being here. He was here to meet with someone, a stranger who was keen to meet with him.

He retrieved the note from inside the envelope, re-examining the finer details of it. He went through the note again as thoroughly as a detective to a murder scene.

It wasn't just about the contents of the note, but everything else about it as well.

The paper was unlined. The author of the letter struggled to write in a straight line. If Tony didn't know better, he would have made the assumption to state the note was written by a young person's hand. There was almost a childish typeset to the note, although the handwriting was set out rather neat.

This hand written letter had been personally delivered and left in Tony's letterbox, sealed in an envelope with only his name, 'Tony,' scrawled across its entire length, all written in capital letters virtually covering the entire length and breadth of the envelope.

Tony had to read the note once again, the message in the letter eerily clear.

The letter read, "Meet me at the park bench in the parkland on Wednesday nine am sharp. You know the place. I will explain all to you then."

And to finish off was a special footnote.

"P.S. - Bring the sunglasses with you."

Tony gazed over the note for a few more seconds before folding the letter back into the envelope and then back into his pocket. The letter had proven a welcome distraction to the depressing emotions he was bathing in only moments before.

He then looked across to his watch. It was eight fifty five am and in five minutes or so, the mystery behind the strange letter would all be revealed.

As soon as Tony shifted his eyes from his watch, he heard her voice, young and sweet.

"Tony it's me," came the voice from behind.

Tony turned to see a young girl, an all too familiar face. He recognised the young girl from the funeral. Back then, her face was superimposed with a demon creature.

Tony instinctively reacted and stood to face off with what he thought to be a demon attacker. Tony faced off with the young girl, he on one side of the park bench and she on the other.

"Tony, it's me!" said the young girl again, trying to calm the situation.

There was a momentary pause.

"It's me, Johnny. I know it's hard to believe, but I can explain."

Tony stopped as if time were frozen still.

"Did you bring the glasses?" asked Allie (Johnny).

Tony didn't nor could he respond for the frightening experience of his previous encounter with Allie was well and truly tattooed in his memories.

Allie asked the question again. Her voice was louder, more directed and this time, demanded a response.

"Did you bring the sunglasses with you?"

Tony cautiously acknowledged the request with a subtle nod of his head. He then reached into his jacket pocket and retrieved the sunglass case.

"Put them on?" Allie asked, but all Tony could manage was a defiant look.

"I cannot spend my time in this park repeating every single request," stated Allie. "Please put them on. You will see that it's me."

After a brief pause, Allie re-assured the message. "It's me Johnny. You'll see!" she stated.

"Please put them on." Allie pleaded again.

Tony lifted the sunglasses to his head and as soon as the lenses were fixed to Tony's eyes, instantly and superimposed on Allie's sweet young face was Johnny's, staring back with his signature cheeky grin.

The stunned look on Tony's face gave it away.

"See, I told you," stated Johnny, speaking through his young female host body.

The vision slowly crept into the working neurons of Tony's brain. The connection between what could be seen with and without the glasses was still a difficult sight to comprehend.

The silence stayed as Tony and the young girl stood staring at one another.

The confused look on Tony's face spoke a thousand words. It was difficult for Tony to utter a single word and so Johnny did the speaking for now.

"I don't know where to begin," said Johnny. "This must be so hard for you," he added. "Please sit down, I don't wish to attract unnecessary attention to our discussion."

"Please," Johnny re-iterated through his young female host body.

A moment later, Tony sat and Johnny (Allie) sat next to him.

"Maybe for now, it will help if you take the glasses off."

"That wouldn't be a bad idea," replied Tony. Tony took his time packing the glasses into the sunglass box and then putting the glass case back into his jacket pocket. By this time a million and one questions had popped into his head.

"How can you, an innocent little girl, be the boy I grew up with? How can you be Johnny?" asked Tony.

"If only you knew," replied Johnny. "You and I, we have travelled the heavens... and the hells. The only reason you don't know it, is because the angels wiped your memories. They wiped your conscious memory, but the subconscious mind stores everything. The memories of our experiences are with you as they are with me."

Tony took his eyes off Allie to look out into the open greenery, looking for Mother Nature to help settle some anxious nerves.

"Search your soul. I really mean it. Dig deep and you will intuitively know I am speaking the truth." Johnny then paused.

All that could be heard was some distant laughter. Two young children accompanied by their mother were playing on some swings in the mid-distance. In the still air there faint laughter and joyous antics could be heard.

Tony watched the children and Johnny (Allie) allowed him the time to do so. After a little while longer Johnny spoke.

"If you have further doubts then ask me anything. Anything only you and Johnny would know and I will answer it for you."

"No. There is no need for that," replied Tony. "This is just a little bit much to take."

"I know it is, but you need to understand, my time is limited here and I have been given an angelic undertaking and without your help, I don't stand a chance."

"Why me?" asked Tony.

"Why us?" replied Johnny.

"I'm sorry, but I don't understand," said Tony.

"Let me fill in the gaps for you," said Johnny. "But before I do, I ask only one thing. The hows and the whys are not important here. That conversation we can save for another time. What is important is that you understand what events have taken place to bring us here today."

Johnny tried to keep the explanation as to the point as possible. He began with an explanation of how Tony and Johnny were drawn into heaven to undertake their angelic mission into the depths of hell.

"We cast God's light right in the middle of Hell Central. I can tell you, Lucifer was pissed off big time," added Johnny.

Johnny did all the talking, rattling off one event after another.

The 'dots' started to connect for Tony. He didn't doubt the facts and as Johnny had suggested, the memories were there. They just needed a little help to surface.

Tony continued to listen.

"Battling that demon in the gothic cathedral was no coincidence. That demon went by the name of Sebastian and he was on the prowl. A high ranking servant answerable to Lucifer himself, he was after both of us and he would have tortured us, he would have killed us in a heartbeat, had he been given the opportunity to do so."

There was a slight pause and then Johnny continued.

"When you take a bit of God's light and transport it deep into hell to set it down smack in the middle of the devil's playground, to shine as a permanent reminder that God's light is ever-present then be prepared for some hellish payback. Like it or not, we took on Lucifer and we came out looking pretty good."

Allie cast a smirk. It had an uncanny resemblance to the way Johnny used to grin at Tony.

"Can you stop that?" Tony stated.

"Stop what?" asked Johnny.

"That grin of yours is so like Johnny's, but not on that face. Not in that body."

"I can't help it, Tony. It's me, Johnny. The little girl who lived in this body was evil and she is now in the heavens being counselled by..."

The conversation appeared to end unnaturally. Tony couldn't let this one go.

"Counselled by whom?" Tony asked.

Johnny hesitantly replied.

"Your grandmother is a special lady, Tony. She helps settle newly arrived souls into heaven. When a soul arrives to heaven which is troubled, disturbed or simply set on evil ways, then your grandmother is never too far away."

Johnny conveyed his message in a way that was genuine and compassionate. Tony enjoyed hearing about his grandmother in that way, but it also led him to ask his next question.

"And what about Mum and Dad?" Tony asked.

"I have seen them, be it briefly, but Tony you need to understand. I had a difficult transition into heaven. Things for me did not go as naturally as they would be expected to be. I have experienced an unholy death and so I have not really been given the chance to settle into heaven's ways and in fact, before I had time to comprehend the realities of my death, I was cast down here to complete another angelic mission."

There was a brief pause before Johnny added, "I have played the part of a little girl and kept up a charade. The lady I call Mum and the house I live in is a house dedicated to the worship of evil. And sometime in the near future, the devil will look to occupy this soul. He has done so many a times before and co-existed with this young girl that was once known as Allie. But now, her soul has gone for good and when I am done, this body will be laid to rest.

"But before I leave this body, I will have to take my final stand with the devil. When Lucifer steps in to use this host body for his evil intentions, then he and I will meet and he will be in for a big surprise, for Allie won't be waiting for him anymore, but I will be!"

Johnny continued to speak as Tony sat there, spellbound.

"I share in Allie's memories. I know what she once knew and I can tell you this much. The devil had plans for this young girl's body. She was going to grow up to rule the world. This girl was going to be wealthy and in a position to influence and make changes on a global scale."

"Not anymore I'm guessing," said Tony.

"You bet!" said Johnny. "Too many have suffered and too much has been lost and if the devil succeeds in his evil ways, then it will have all been for nothing. Listen to me, Tony, this goes beyond you and me, there is far too much at stake here and for better or for worse, I need your help."

Tony was numb, his eyes set to the mid-distance again. The playing children and their mother had left a little while back and for the time being, the parkland was getting busier with other young families coming out to enjoy some mid-week playtime activity.

Tony then looked across to Allie. "I'm not sure how I can help."

"Well, you can and besides, if you had been a victim of a heinous crime. If you had previously suffered a violence so unholy knowing now that something else was required—that some kind of costly payback must be made to put things right."

Johnny (Allie) stood and walked away from the park bench. A few steps later, Johnny turned to face Tony.

Tony kept to his silence. There was anger in his heart and determination in his eyes, the type of determination a heavyweight champion goes into the boxing ring with on a title fight. The next words to be spoken would be hers.

Tony shifted his eyes and for now, the scenery of the parkland greenery kept him pre-occupied until Allie was ready to speak again.

A little time later Allie walked up to the park bench and positioned herself in front of Tony. She knelt on the lawn before him, her on the ground, him seated on the park bench, so their eyes were locked in on one another.

The strain of the pain was there. The type of look one gives when their soul is burdened with suffering and loss.

Tony could see that much. He could feel the deeply seated sorrow within himself and he could see the hurt and pain come through in the eyes of his friend.

They had both endured a lot.

"I can't do this alone, Tony," said the young female voice.

Having Johnny appear on this Earth in a different human form would take some getting used to, but Tony would be there for his friend.

In heaven and on Earth and to the depths of hell and back, Tony would be there for his friend.

Chapter Thirty-six
The Final Encounter

The scene was set.

Tony managed to talk the new pastor of Johnny's church into allowing him to have some private time. Just Tony, sitting all alone in a suburban church, or at least that was what the pastor believed.

Tony, on the other hand, had a hidden agenda. The trap for Lucifer and his evil doers had been set.

Tony stood in the churchyard courtyard for a moment longer. The night time sky was clear, scattered with twinkling stars and a moon that was only happy to expose a slither for which to shine for the people of the Earth. All was silent except for the handful of chirping crickets. They couldn't manage to get their harmonies together and yet chirped away, all holding true to their individual melodies.

Tony looked at his watch. It was almost eight pm. He walked inside leaving the church doors ajar.

Tony sat patiently as time passed by. A little time later, Tony looked at his watch again; it was closer to eight thirty and that observation made his heart pound a little harder than before. Tony stood from the aisle altar seat and walked closer to the church door entrance. Tony, for a short time, jumped side to side and up and down, as would an athlete, warming up before a sprint race. He needed to shake off his nervous energy.

Through the space between the doors he saw her approaching alone. Allie (Johnny) was steadily making her way towards the entrance. She drew nearer. Tony stopped what he was doing, and positioned himself as to not be seen by any outside prying eyes.

He took in a slow deep breath and exhaled just as slowly. The time to put plan into action was only a minute or so away.

Tony stayed close to the inside of the door, but remained hidden.

Allie would be near the door soon.

Outside and unknown to Tony, Angela approached the holy property and quickly hid in the shadows of neighbouring big trees and shrubbery. She watched her little Allie walk towards the church entrance.

Allie (Johnny) hesitantly paused from outside the basilica door.

Allie heard a faint whisper from the other side of the wooded entrance.

"Is she here? Is she watching?" asked an anxious Tony.

"You mustn't give it away. Stick to the plan and keep silent. If my so called mother suspects a trap then she won't follow me into the church and Lucifer won't try and repossess me at the critical moment," whispered Allie (Johnny.).

Immediately after this soft, discreet conversation, Allie looked around to her mother who signalled by waving her to go in.

Allie (Johnny) walked inside, only to see Tony standing nearby. Allie quickly blurted out to Tony. "My mother will be here soon. We don't have a lot of time to prepare."

Angela remained outside for a little while longer.

Inside, Tony and Allie (Johnny) rushed to the front altar. They stood where a priest would normally stand, facing out to his congregation.

While waiting, Johnny (Allie) rushed over his plans again. There was no room for error.

Angela came in moments later and approached Tony and Allie.

"Allie, get away from him," demanded Angela of her daughter. "We have a little surprise for you, young man," Angela said, with a cheeky grin impressed across her sinister face.

"It is so nice of you to give up your personal time so that we may have some private time in this house of prayer," Angela said and then laughed out aloud, her wicked ridden voice echoing throughout this holy place of worship.

And as suddenly as that, Angela's eyes went distant and stayed like that for a short while.

Eddie Georgonicas

A moment or two later, Angela snapped out of her trance-like state, directing her conversation to her daughter.

"Sweetheart, he is here. You know what to do."

Allie (Johnny) stepped to a side corner of the church, putting some space between her and Tony.

All the attention was on Allie as her eyeballs rolled back, leaving the whites of her eyes staring out blankly into nothingness.

Angela, for certain, would have been under the impression that Lucifer was entering her daughter's soul. Tony knew better. The battle for good and evil had commenced.

Tony let his anger surface.

"It is you who is in for a surprise, you evil witch. Your satanic lord is going to have a little meeting with some of heavens finest, I believe."

Angela's face instantly shocked and shortly after, Allie's body begun to convulse. Her body was in a type of an epileptic seizure. Her soul was housing a number of spiritual guests; spirits from opposing sides.

Angela stepped forward in a motherly attempt to protect her daughter.

Tony drew his right hand high. It was not in his nature to do so, nor would he ever strike out at the opposite gender, but in this instance, there was a valid reason for it and there was no hesitation in his action.

He swung his open palm down hard and fast and slapped Angela to the ground.

"While I stand and breathe, you will not get near your daughter," stated Tony.

Angela got up from the ground. A second's pause and she ran for Tony, charging at him like an angry bull, screaming out for all to hear.

Tony side stepped her, slapping her oncoming face with the open palm of his left hand. The force of the slap combined with her forward momentum and resulting fall was enough to knock Angela out cold.

She lay there motionless whilst a few feet away, Allie's body convulsed in an endless seizure.

"You are free to do what you need to do. Be strong, my friend," Tony spoke the words to Johnny's (Allie's) spirit. Words that Johnny would never hear, but words of comfort none-the-less.

205

~ * ~

Inside Allie's body, on a spiritual level, Lucifer was in for the biggest surprise.

Face to face with Archangels Michael, Gabriel and angel Raphael and behind the demonic trio, Johnny standing there, strong and defiant.

All four were there to greet Lucifer and surprise him they did.

"You!" shouted Lucifer in response to the sight of Johnny.

Michael shuffled forward a little, enough to block out Lucifer's line of sight of Johnny.

The angelic trio stood firm and in reply, Lucifer held his ground.

It was a silent face off; one that drew out for an uncomfortably long time.

Johnny remained in the shadows of his angelic friends. To not look upon the dark lord again was fine enough for him.

Angel Raphael and Archangel Gabriel moved closer. Soon, the three angels stood in one straight line.

"Your reign of terror on this planet is over," Michael stated in no uncertain terms.

It was easy to see how Lucifer did not want to give up all that he had worked so hard to achieve. But even Lucifer had the smarts to know when to tastefully retreat.

There could be no point into putting further energies into the unwinnable.

"I will see you all in hell," were Lucifer's final words to the angels and Johnny. He screamed them out with a sickening screech before vanishing for good.

~ * ~

Angela's eyes fluttered and she awoke. A second or two to gather her senses and it hit her psyche harder than the previous slap to the face. The look on her face said it all. Tony knew it and by the looks of it, Angela could sense it as well.

Her evil lord was gone. Her daughter's soul was no longer in possession of the body. Everything that stood before Angela was a doer of good and all things holy.

All signs and sensations of evil had been abolished.

Angela looked around. She appeared to be assessing her situation. Tony knew it and Angela was about to discover that all hope for her evil plan was lost.

As quick as a flash, Tony was surrounded in feelings of a holy victory whilst Angela's eyes swarmed with looks of despair and defeat.

It didn't take much longer to realise there was nothing further for her to do.

Angela turned and fled the church, running out of there as fast as she could manage.

"And don't you ever show your face in here again," shouted Tony to the back of Angela as she continued to flee, never stopping and never looking back.

~ * ~

The battle was over and good had triumphed over evil.

Lucifer was on a one way ticket back to Hell Central. In time, he would undoubtedly be back to his evil ways, but at least the people of the Earth could now live their lives without the fear of one day being ruled and influenced by Satan's sinister ways.

Allie (Johnny) was worn out down on Earth. Her young body had endured a lot.

"I must go, Tony, but before I do, there are some I would like you to meet."

Suddenly, ghostly apparitions formed, standing only a few feet in front of Johnny and Tony. All in all, there were seven formations floating in front, too hazy and out of focus to tell exactly what or who they were.

Johnny introduced them and as he did, two of the ghostly apparitions took a much clearer, crisper form. Phasing into view was the archangel Gabriel and angel Raphael.

Tony's look of amazement was instantaneous; their sheer beauty hit his eyes like the glare of the sun. Raphael and Gabriel stood there with their wings tucked behind them.

Johnny spoke. "These are but two of our angelic guides. These angels have been our protectors, our heavenly guides, our friends. I'd like to introduce you to the archangel Gabriel and the angel Raphael."

Gabriel and Raphael spoke no words and simply acknowledged the introduction with the classical angelic salute. With one elbow bent, and closed fist held firm up against their chest, they bowed as they thumped their chest as a sign of respect.

At that moment, in phased Archangel Michael, his ghostly apparition stepping forward; crisp and clear, he took his position in front of his angelic friends. Archangel Michael had centre stage as he stood up close and personal with Tony.

"May I introduce you to Archangel Michael," said Johnny.

"Pleased to meet you," said Tony.

"No it is I who am honoured to meet with you," said Michael.

Tony's face lit up.

Michael extended his wings. They majestically stretched out as far as they could go. Tony had to shuffle back a little to take in the full panoramic view of an archangel and his stretched out, all white, swan-like wings.

"We all have our angelic guides; an angel who takes a special interest in our lives and where we are heading. An angel who guides us when life gets off track," said Allie (Johnny). "And although quite a few angels have taken an interest in us, Tony, Archangel Michael has been entrusted to guide us through our lifetimes," added Johnny (Allie).

"You may not comprehend what you have done for the angels in heaven, young man, but we are eternally grateful to you and your friend Johnny," stated Michael.

A cheer rang out from behind Michael.

Gabriel and Raphael could be heard cheering away. "Here, Here!"

"Here, Here!" they cheered again.

"There's a few more special people you also need to say hello to," said Johnny and as his introduction came to a close, Pam, Charlie and Mary phased into view.

A mixture of sadness and happiness washed over Tony. The confusion overwhelmed the young man as he quickly covered his eyes; the tears flowed and the shoulders heaved. The time to release all that emotion, all that tension had finally arrived at the sight of his deceased parents and grandmother.

Tony had the time he needed to get over what he needed to get over.

A little while later, Tony opened his eyes, but all was gone. The world around him went dark. Although inside the church, not a speck of light could be seen.

Tony could hear something dripping and then an unexplainable cold rushed through his body. He shivered, if only for a second or two and then immediately he noticed the surface below him felt damp.

"Johnny, are you here?" Tony asked with a panic in his voice.

"We are all here, Tony. You needn't worry. All is safe inside these walls," Johnny replied.

"It would mean so much for me to hold you again, sweetheart," said his mother, Mary, her sweet voice echoing in the black of darkness.

His mother's voice felt so comforting.

"We are so proud of you, son," added his father, Charlie.

His father's voice had always been there to provide him with a sense of accomplishment.

In that minute, Tony stood taller and stronger for it.

The ghostly entities let the darkness hang for a little while longer and then slowly, the lights of the church flickered for a little while before resuming their normal brightness.

Eagerly, Tony sought out Johnny and turned to see Allie's body slumped to the ground. Tony rushed over to the body and then kneeled down, gently shaking the still, young female host body.

"Johnny, are you okay?" he asked instinctively. "Johnny!" he exclaimed.

"I'm over here," answered Johnny. Johnny had now returned to his ghostly form. He'd left Allie's body as he had said would happen, once the job of defeating Lucifer was over.

"We will take care of this, Tony. We walk away.if we can't rehabilitate Angela in heaven then we will allow earthly laws to see to her punishment. As far as the authorities are concerned, Allie's death will be linked to her mother and she will be sentenced accordingly. This will be her cross to bear."

Pam walked towards her grandson. Her ghostly presence had Tony mesmerised.

"Live life to the fullest, my sweet and dear grandson. Death is merely a time apart. In heaven we shall meet again; when you have done your time on Earth, then we will be here for you in heaven, ready to pick up where we last left off."

"You have a full life ahead of you," added Mary.

"Live it. Live it. Live it," stated Johnny.

The message washed over Tony like a cold shower. In the moment when that icy water hits your warm skin and you shiver until you adjust, at the very least, in the best way you can. This is what it felt like for Tony.

The message was well understood. It may take a bit more time to fully comprehend, but it was well understood.

"You must leave. The authorities will be here soon," said Charlie.

Tony hesitated until Johnny spoke out again.

"You must go now. Before the police arrive."

Tony left, but not before he returned the largest of smiles for all to see. A smile that symbolised that no matter what life throws at you. All of its ups and all of its downs; take life one step at a time, tackle the challenges head on and believe that for good and for bad, there is always a lesson to be learnt.

And above all, with the one life that you are given, whatever your chosen path and destiny… always live the life you have to the fullest.

From the Author

For more information, please visit www.eddiegeorgonicas.com.

Also by the Author
at
Rogue Phoenix Press

Spiritual Dreams of a Heavenly War
Book One in the Anarchy of Angels Trilogy

Tony's life has had its challenges and Johnny has always been there for him. Two young men, inseparable and as close as any two best friends could be. The Angels have been observing them for a long time. There is a plan in the making and they need their help. Every rule in Heaven will be broken in order to achieve this ultimate objective. And as a result, two young friends will die well before their intended times in order to help the Angelic intent. Selfish? Maybe but then again... Heaven gets more than what it bargained for. And Heaven is in more trouble that it lets on. The boys will come to see this as they go deep into the land of "fire and brimstone." They will come to venture where no Angel dare.

A Heavenly Interception
Book Two in the Anarchy of Angels Trilogy

The Dark One is on the rampage, a demonic beast is on the prowl. He stalks two boys across two continents unintentionally playing a game of "cat and mouse". But of utmost significance is his need to move around the Earth incognito. And what better way than to rid a human shell of its soul and then "step in" to take it over. The boys will be forced into defending their lives as well as the lives of those innocent souls that are with them. The final showdown is behind the closed doors of the famous Gothic Church located in the city of Cologne, Germany. It is here where Angelic Intention, Hellish influence, Earthly friendships, a psychic medium and an innocent German family all link together for one last time.